I0717711

ZERACH'S AWAKENING

NOEL MORRISON

ISBN   978-1-970160-80-2   Ebook
ISBN   978-1-970160-81-9   Paperback

EC Publishing LLC
11100 SW 93rd Court Road, Suite 10-215
Ocala, Florida 34481-5188, USA

Ordering Information:
Quantity sales. Special discounts are available on quantity purchases by corporations, associations, and others. For details, contact the publisher at the address above.

www.ecpublishingllc.com
info@ecpublishingllc.com
+1 (352) 234-6201

Printed in the United States of America

PROLOGUE

Zerach is frightened. He hears the voices coming from the spheres. He tries to block them out but he can't.

'You must listen, Zerach. We've waited such a long time for another human to have your special gifts.'

He flings himself on his bed *and covers his* head *with his pillow but they are relentless. 'You are one of the Chosen,' they sing. 'There are three others. 'Three boys and one girl. Together you will make the perfect four.'*

Zerach doesn't want to be chosen. He wants to be left alone; to play football, *go skateboarding, and hang out with his friends. 'Forget the foolish game,' they chant. 'They will distract you. These distractions will make it harder for you when you are called.'*

'Called for what?' he shouts but they don't answer him.

Although Zerach's eyes are closed he can see the spheres shimmer. They grow brighter. They fill the room with The Knowledge. It is inside him. It has been there since his birth. Zerach thinks of it as his curse. The spheres are liars. It is not a gift. It is an illness.

Night creeps into his room. He watches the shadows that are cast on the wall by the Venetian blinds. He needs to sleep but with his sleep comes the Dreams. He sees the vague shapes of the other three who like him are known to the spheres.

They have been in his Dreams which started on his fourth birthday. Each night he sees them but they flee. Like him, they don't want to heed The Call.

Moonlight peeps through his window. Soon the spheres will begin to sing the song of the stars. They have waited for centuries. The time has come.

Their bliss is heard throughout the Universe. Their pure harmony is dazzling and the atoms dance in joy. Soon. Soon.

CHAPTER ONE

Zerach

'Benjamin? Is that Zerach?' asked his wife Esther. He put down the research papers he was reading and hopes that she's mistaken. He walked to the bottom of the stairs and listened. As he did Esther leant forward, her body rigid and alert for the slightest noise. He turned briefly and watched her. She twisted her wedding ring around her finger in a continuous loop. He tried not to look, or worse, to say something, but he knew that he could not mention it.

Her finger was swollen and painful. She had rubbed off the outer layers of her skin. Now, she had an angry red scab that nothing can cure. It wept constantly but she was unable stop herself. He saw her wince, but she continued to turn it. Around and around it went; an endless circle of pain.

He longed to hold her. If only he could hold her hand in the Dreadful circling might stop. He knew, however, that he couldn't. Everything he had tried had failed.

'I can't hear anything. Are you sure you heard something?' he asked.

'He's talking in his sleep. Surely you can hear him?' she asked. Benjamin knew that he must sound calm. It is vital that he sounds rational and reassuring. He breathed in softly through his nose.

Gained a few seconds. It is essential that he adopts the right tone. Even the tiniest change of timbre in his voice will alert her.

'I'm sure he's fine,' he says, pleased that his voice has struck the right note. 'I'll go check. He could be talking to one of his friends on his phone.'

'He knows that he's not allowed to use his phone after ten,' she replies. Her voice is soft but he has heard her hint of churlishness. 'Esther, he's a teenager,' he said gently.

'Benjamin please. Go and check. Then I can at least try to relax.' He knows that she'll never relax. Not until their son is cured. He knows, as she does, that there is no cure. The best they can hope for is to hold back the damn that makes him ill. Esther, he knows, still needs the false comfort of a cure. To believe that Zerach will return as he once was; happy, sociable and full of wit. 'If he's talking on his phone I'll speak to him. Okay?'

He stood outside Zerach's bedroom. Can he hear something or is he imagining it? He heard a voice: a voice that sound nothing like Zerach's. Alarmed he opens the door. His son is lying tangled in his bed covers. Perspiration flooded down his face. His eyes stare at the empty ceiling. Zerach is both present and absent; as if he is drawn into a different realm.

Benjamin's too shocked to move. He stood, helpless and terrified as he listens to the voice coming from Zerach's mouth. They are garbled, but occasionally, he can make out a few words. Benjamin forced himself to move. He knelt down by the bed. Should he wake him? Could that cause another psychotic episode that has plagued his son in the past?

He hesitated. He wished that he could ask Esther what he should do. He knows he can't. Four months ago, Zerach started hearing voices. When Benjamin had first told Esther she had become hysterical and now took antidepressants and Valium. Far too much Valium. He pretends that he doesn't know.

He touched Zerach on his shoulder. He felt the heat that emanates from his body. It is unnatural. That much he knew. No-one can have a temperature so high. It radiates from him like a flame. Benjamin hugged him. Rocked him as he did when his son was a baby. Again, he wondered if he should risk waking him. Ask what had happened? No, he decided. Better to let him sleep.

He stumbled down the stairs. At the bottom of the staircase he held onto the banister. He needed to steady himself, to gain a few seconds of time. He must, he told himself, act as if Zerach is alright. He will check him later. Persuade Esther to go to bed and say that he must stay up to finish the exam papers that are due back to his students by the end of the week. He forced himself to clear his mind and to prepare himself for the lies.

Esther sat as he has left her. She has been cast in stone. Statue like, she had waited. He walked to her and kissed the top of her head. She tenses. He knows that soon, she will take another Valium. It will be her fifth or sixth for the day. She is allowed three. She knows that they are addictive. She is indifferent to what she is told.

'Is he, all right?' she asked.

'He's fine. A bit restless but he'll soon settle. I'll check on him later.'

'I need to see him. What if he's getting sick again?' He saw the look of terror on her face. He knows that if she heard Zerach talking in such a bizarre way she would unravel. 'Let me make you a cup of Camomile tea. Then I'll go and check him again. If I have any doubt I'll let you know.'

'I'll have the tea but I'm not going to bed until I see him.'

'Fine,' he procrastinates. 'I'll let it brew the way you like it. How does that sound?'

She says nothing but nodded her head and looked up to the stair case. He went to the kitchen and switched on the kettle. While he waited for it to boil he reached up into the cupboard. He edged his fingers closer to where she has hidden some of the tablets. He takes two. Twenty milligrams. A high dose, on top of the extra that she has taken but he can't allow her to see Zerach. What if the voices returned? She wouldn't cope but he's prepared to pay the price for feeling guilty.

He crushed the tablets and mixed them with warm water. He

added the white tablets to her mug, put in two tea bags and let it steep. He waited for ten minutes. He added honey. It is more than she liked, but he must disguise the bitter taste of the Valium. He stirred it vigorously and slowly walked back to the lounge.

'Lost the tea bags again?'

'Yes. I can never find the bloody things. I always get the tins mixed up. I accidently made an Earl Grey tea and had to make another one.' He handed her the cup. She sniffed it suspiciously. 'Well at least it's Camomile. You got that bit right.' He saw her face soften. She reached out her hand and he took it in his.

'Esther try to stop worrying so much. He's been fine for four months. Why should he start having the Dreams and hearing voices again? Dr Michal said he's doing very well.' He knows he sounds convincing. He is not a natural liar but has learnt its craft. He can conjure the fake tones that ring of truthfulness.

'I'm still terrified that it'll start again. I know that he's improved. I used to think I was strong. Then, when he started hearing voices, I felt so hopeless. He believed, really believed, that the voices told him he had a special role to play in the world. Thank God for Dr Michal and the medication she prescribed. I know this sounds selfish but I can't go through it again. I don't have the strength.'

'Well that's in the past. We're both a bit on edge. It's perfectly understandable. Now Drink your tea.' Dutifully she sipped. He waited. At last she finished. She sat silently and has mercifully stopped twisting her ring in its cruel circles. Scabs have formed, been broken and formed again. 'I know Camomile tea relaxes you but now I can barely stay awake.' She hesitated. 'Do you promise me that he wasn't saying anything?'

'Not a word.'

She rises slowly to her feet. 'I don't think I've got the energy to walk up the stairs. I'll sleep down here in the spare bedroom. Thanks for the tea.' He kisses her goodnight. Can he deceive her indefinitely? He must ring Dr Michal again. She'll know what to do.

He tries to grade a few more assignments but he's too distracted. How long should he wait for the Valium to start working? He forces himself to wait for fifteen minutes. He went to the spare room and listened. Her breathing was deep and regular. She was, overmedicated but nevertheless, the Valium had done what he'd planned.

It was late but Dr Michal had said to ring her no matter what time it was. He scrolled through his contacts in his phone but suddenly changed his mind. Zerach would be fine, he told himself. One small incident didn't mean that Zerach had relapsed. Besides, his son was already having weekly sessions with Dr Michal and adding to his burden would be too much. He would wait. This was not the time to panic. He needed to be logical and calm. It was the advice he always gave to his maths students and one which he now needed to heed for himself.

CHAPTER TWO

Benjamin climbed into bed and turned off the bedside lamp. He couldn't get the sound of Zerach's voice out of his head. He knew that it was a symptom of his schizophrenia but that didn't explain how his son had sounded. The longer he thought about it the more agitated he became. He turned on his light and went to Zerach's room. He waited for a few moments but it was clear that he was asleep. Relieved, he returned to his bedroom and sat reading a book that Esther had left on her bedside cabinet. He was not a reader but he forced himself to try to follow the intricate plot of Esther's favourite author.

He struggled through to chapter three then tossed the book on the floor. He rolled over and turned off his light. He lay listening to the ticking of the clock-a sound that Esther found so reassuring. He closed his eyes and lay there as each tick measured out the seconds.

He started to count the ticking of the clock. Any distraction, no matter how puerile was better than the image of Zerach and the eerie voice that he'd made. As the hours passed he knew that sleep was impossible.

Wearily he climbed out of bed and made his way to Zerach's room. He opened the door. His son was asleep and breathing deeply. He thought how young he looked. A wave of nostalgia forced him to stop for a moment. He can't, he tells himself, allow the luxury of such an emotion.

He looked again at Zerach and tried to stay focused on the present moment. In spite of his resolve not to revisit the past he was unable to stop himself. Time had not lessened the vividness of **what had happened when Zerach had first shown signs of his illness.** He **wished that the memory** would fade but it was like a film: a spool waiting to be played the moment that he thought about the past.

***

It had started when Zerach had just turned sixteen. He was, they had both thought, a young man, who like most teenagers, could be challenging but these moments were rare. True, Zerach could be moody and sometimes unpredictable but this too, they felt, fitted within the normal parameters for a young man **of his age.**

Zerach was an outstanding student who had the ability to excel without seeming to try. He was not arrogant, unlike some of his peers, who like Zerach had been classified as being gifted. They were proud of him. He was loved and had been nurtured by his Jewish parents whose heritage and religious beliefs Zerach had embraced. What they had not known, could not have known, was that Zerach's brain chemistry was not as it should be. His illness had **remained dormant as it patiently waited to emerge.** Then it had struck.

One that morning Benjamin and Esther had been sitting in the lounge room as the morning sun peeped through the window. It had been a hot summer but Esther had planted numerous shade trees that filtered out the sun and gave the room a sense of mellowness they loved.

Benjamin was about to go and make them both a coffee when Zerach had slowly came down the stairs. He was still in his boxer shorts and his hair ballooned out from his head like a golden halo. They looked at him and smiled. They were surprised to see him just in his boxer shorts. He was self-conscious about his changing body and of the awkwardness that puberty had thrust on him. As they looked, it became obvious that there was something wrong. His face looked different. His gait, as he carefully took one step at a time, was stilted and unnatural. He looked at them as if they were strangers.

Benjamin and Esther stood up and looked at each other in confusion. As they walked closer to Zerach their original emotions disappeared to be replaced by one of fear. Zerach was whispering and looking over his shoulder as if someone was behind him. He nodded to himself and clumsily sat down on the bottom step waiting as if he were an actor listening for his cue. He cleared his throat and spoke.

'I've decided that I'm not going to synagogue anymore. I don't need it. Like all religions it pretends to know the truth when it doesn't.'

'Zerach where on earth is this coming from? asked Esther. She went to him and tried to sit next to him. He moved away and held out his hands in front of him as if he was a prophet.

'You can't change my mind. No matter what you do or say will make any difference.' **Esther's** shocked face looked at Benjamin beseeching him to say something. But he, unlike his son, struggled to speak. How should he respond, he asked himself? He knew of course that Zerach's strange behaviour was as a result of what had happened the previous night. He wanted to sound supportive and reassuring but in spite of knowing that he was doing the wrong thing he was unable to keep the hurt from his voice.

'But you have always loved going. It's part of our religious heritage and culture.'

'It may be part of what you choose to believe but it's no longer mine. Now I know better.'

'Why now Zerach? Has something happened to make you change your mind so suddenly?' Esther asked.

'The voices told me. I know now that the synagogue is irrelevant.'

'But what about your friends? Nearly all of them go to synagogue. You've known them most of your life. Are you going to stop seeing them?' Esther looked at him as if she couldn't comprehend what she'd heard. Up to now Zerach had been so proud when he and his Jewish friends had had their Bar Mitzvah's.

'You studied so hard to remember the words you had to say before you went to the ceremony. I remember how committed you were. After we came home you said that you were thinking of becoming a Rabbi. And now this! How can you sit there and say these terrible things? I know that you've not been well but you've been fine. I don't understand.'

'I've started my journey. My friends are not part of it.'

'Journey? Journey? What are you talking about?'

'I can't tell you. You have not been chosen. I have. This is my journey not yours.' He turned around, gave them a pitying look and went upstairs to his room.

'He's relapsed, hasn't he? asked Esther. Benjamin looked uncomfortable and struggled to know how to respond to her question? What if he told her that he had heard Zerach talking to the voices, or more alarming still, that they appeared to be talking to their son? He should have told her what he'd seen the night before. He shouldn't have tried to shield her from what she was entitled to know. Even If she reacted badly it was not his role to deprive her of what was happening to their son.

'I should have told you last night but I didn't want to worry you.'

'Told me what? If you've hidden something from me about Zerach I'm not sure that I can forgive you.'

'I'm sorry Esther. It wasn't about hiding what happened. I was trying to protect you.'

'Protect me? Protect me? I think the world's moved on from knights saving damsels in distress, don't you?'

'I don't think you're being fair. I was trying to protect you because I know that you're struggling.'

'And you're not I suppose?'

'You know I am but I'm not taking medication and you are. I thought that any extra stress might make you . . .' he trailed off uncertain of how to continue.

'Benjamin,' she said enunciating each syllable as if it were a bullet, 'I know that I've been prescribed medication but that's not a reason to deceive me.'

He had to tell her. He had to say that he knew that she was

incrementally increasing her Valium and now she was well over her dosage rate. Whatever he said it would be wrong but he had to diffuse the situation. They could work together and not declare a state of war. He watched her as she stood so close to him that he felt almost threatened. He took a step back, and as he did, she took a step towards him.

'Don't you dare do that! You're my husband. If I can't stand close to you than we've got a bigger problem that I thought.'

'What problem?'

'Us Benjamin. Can't you see what it's doing to us?'

'I thought we were fine given what's happened. I know things are hard but this new development is something I had no idea of.'

'I think life is easier for you. Because you're a mathematician everything's is so neat and orderly. The rest of us see the world the way it is: messy and confusing. Life's more complex than mathematical formulas.'

'Esther, I think you're projecting your feelings onto me. I'm not a robot. I worry. I weep. I sometimes despair.'

He saw the look of shock and surprise on her face and he waited for another barrage of words. She moved back and looked at him. He braced himself urging himself to sound calm but not too calm. Whatever he did or did not do was riddled with risk and he suddenly felt exhausted. It was hard enough coping with Zerach but he had never expected this.

'Despair? You? You felt despair?' she asked softly.

'Yes. Despair and you have it too don't you?' They stood there as if lost: two actors in a play who had forgotten their lines and were waiting for their prompts.

'I suppose.'

'Esther you're not on antidepressants for nothing. You're suffering. I know that you've been taking too many Valium. I know it's hard but in a job like yours you can't afford to make any mistakes. If you're over medicated who knows what might happen?'

He saw that she wanted to object. To deny what he had said and rail against him but she appeared too surprised to answer. 'Can we please sit down Esther and I'll make us a coffee and we can start again?' She nodded and he quickly made the coffee and handed it to her. She took it meekly and blew on it as the steam rose about her.

'Too hot?'

'It'll be fine.' He looked at her finger and saw that it was bleeding. She must have been twisting her ring around as they had argued and he felt his guilt flush to his face.

'Don't feel guilty Benjamin.'

'How did you know . . .?'

'What you were going to say?'

He smiled. She knew him to well. He reached over and touched her bleeding finger. 'That looks so sore.'

'It is but forget it. We need to talk about our son. Why has this started again? I thought that he was doing so well. I'm not sure I can go through it again. It doesn't seem fair. It's as if we were given a miracle then it's been snatched away.' She sat on the bottom step and put her head in her hands and started to weep.

It was not the type of tears that could bring emotional relief. These were the tears of despair. Benjamin sat next to her and put his arms around her. He felt her shoulders shuddering and her crying seemed as if it would never stop. She started keening and he held her tighter and at last she stopped.

She searched her pockets for a tissue but couldn't find one. He passed her his handkerchief and she wiped her eyes. 'Sorry. The last thing you need to deal with is me falling apart.'

'Crying out of love for your son is a perfectly natural thing to do. I'll give Dr Michal a call. I'll ring her from my study.'

He went into the study and dialled her number. He needed to tell Dr Michal about Zerach's strange behaviour from the previous night but he didn't want his wife to hear what he said.

'Yes.'

'Hi Michal. It's Benjamin.'

'Hi. Is everything okay? You sound a bit stressed.'

'Zerach has started hearing voices again.'

'When did they start?'

'We're not really sure but I heard him last night. He seemed to be going okay and this morning he announced that he wasn't going to synagogue anymore because the voices apparently said it's not necessary.'

'Has he been taking his medication?'

'Yes. He was doing so well. That's what's got us rattled. How can it happen like that?'

'There are a number of possibilities. I'll need to see him. I can come in early tomorrow. Can you get him here by half past eight?'

'Yes. I'll make sure of it.'

'Good. I know it's easy for me to say but try not to worry too much. It's more than likely that he needs him meds increased but I don't want to pre-empt anything at this stage. Can you get him here by then?'

'Yes. He'll come whether he wants to or not. This has to be fixed. Thanks for putting him in. I'm sure you're very busy.'

'Not so busy that I can't make time for Zerach. I'll see you tomorrow.'

'Thanks again Michal. I really appreciate this and everything that you've done.'

'Sorry Benjamin but my first patient has arrived. I have to go. Take care.'

It was Dr Michal who had diagnosed Zerach as suffering from schizophrenia. He was prescribed Zyprexa and it had stabilised him. How wrong they were, he thought bitterly.

CHAPTER THREE

Benjamin and Esther had dressed for Synagogue and though neither of them spoke they each knew what the other was thinking. Could they get Zerach to change his mind?

'Do you think . . .'

'Yes, Benjamin I do think we need to try. Perhaps he's had a change of heart. Adolescent boys say all sorts of things then the next day they seem to change their mind as if they never mentioned it in the first place.'

'It could backfire.'

'Yes, Ben it could. But so could just giving up on his faith. It was his faith, our faith and our ancestors that got us through the holocaust and to throw it away as if it's nothing it's . . . it' s . . . 'She tried to continued but couldn't talk. For her son to throw away the very foundations of their family and their culture that had endured for thousands of years was devastating.

She started to weep. Her German ancestors had been killed by the Nazis and she held on to her Jewishness with a love and passion that she'd thought Zerach would never abandon.

'Let me see how is this morning shall I? Then together we may be able to work something out.'

'Benjamin. What's to work out? Either he comes or he doesn't. Not much working out involved I would have thought.'

'We'll both go up and see him. We owe it to him and to ourselves to do something. This is too important to ignore. We are Jewish and so is he. He needs to understand that.'

They looked at each other and at last Esther nodded and they **started to climb** the stairs as if they were going to the guillotine. They **were not prepared to let him discard his faith** as if it **were** inconsequential.

Still they waited. The silence was full of their fear and both of them hoped that the other would take the lead. That way, if anything went wrong then they could avert the blame. Both of them were ashamed of their emotions but were honest enough to acknowledge its presence.

At last Esther nodded and she pulled back her shoulders and took a deep breath. She **took the first step and began climbing** the stairs with a confidence that amazed Benjamin and he followed **like a** cowardly lamb needing to be **lead.**

She hesitated for a few seconds and then took Benjamin's hand and gave it a squeeze. He squeezed back and knew that she was aware of how he had judged himself. They listened outside of Zerach's door and hearing nothing they went in.

Zerach lay on his back looking peaceful. His face looked so innocent. **There was no hint** that something might be wrong. They looked at each other and they knew that they wouldn't wake him. Benjamin gently shut the door. On the way to the synagogue they were unable to speak. Part of them was missing.

CHAPTER FOUR

Zerach woke as the sun shimmered onto his mirror which he has placed so that it caught the sun's morning rays. He liked rising early. He thought that his mirror was special. He and his father had found it at the dump one Saturday.

'But what,' his father had said genuinely bemused, 'on earth do you need a mirror in your room? There's one in the hallway and as far as I recall the one in the bathroom seems to have all of its working parts.'

His dad had smiled, waiting for some sort of witty repartee from his son but Zerach had said nothing. How, he'd wondered, could he explain that the mirror's gilded edges, festooned with swirls of colour around its edges representing the twelve signs of the zodiac would appeal to an adolescent boy? It had nothing to do with his vanity. He couldn't care less about how he looked.

He was genuinely puzzled when the female students and a couple of the male students would look at him, admiring his face and physique. When he looked at himself in the mirror to brush his hair he saw a face that was solemn and had well proportioned features. He was unaware that he possessed that rare genetic fluke that gave his face its perfect proportions. He never exercised and thought that working out was boring. It was his mind that mattered, nothing else was important.

It was of course precisely his mind that Dr Michal was interested in. During his first session with her she had asked him a series of questions. He'd told her only enough of the truth to sound convincing. She had listened and had arranged another session. Like the first they'd chatted about what he was experiencing. He had known what her diagnosis would be. He had **googgled** his symptoms and it too, agreed with Dr Michal's diagnosis.

After three appointments his parents had been asked to come with him for a "family conference." He'd been amused at the euphemism knowing full well what they were about to be told.

They'd entered her office with its beautiful paintings that adorned most of the walls. The room was comfortable but functional except for a small statue of a winged creature that was so black it looked as if it had been created by a genius. It stood about twenty centimetres high and its wings were half unfurled and each feather was burnished to bright perfection. Its face was extraordinary. It was beautiful but there was something unsettling about it. Beneath the beauty and magnificence of the statue there was something else – something that couldn't be named. It seemed to indicate that, whilst the statue was aware of its beauty, the price it had paid had been too high.

Zerach wanted to say something about the statue. He saw his parents looking at it as intently as he was, but they too, said nothing. Finally, Dr Michal smiled and gestured that they should sit.

'Beautiful isn't it?' Dr Michal got up from her chair and touched the statue. Her face had a look of reverence that surprised Zerach. He was not an expert on human behaviour, after all that was Dr Michal's job, but was it normal to revere a statue?

Dr Michal ran her finger along the length of it lingering for a moment as she touched its face. As if sensing Zerach's puzzlement she added: 'I'm a bit of a fan of sculpture, especially one as old as this.'

'How old is it?' Zerach asked.

'About two thousand years. I'm not an expert but the person who gave it to me said that I had to take great care of it. He was most adamant about that. I thought it was Egyptian but I think it may be even earlier than that.'

'Did they make statues so beautiful before the Egyptians?' Esther asked puzzled as to why they were sitting around discussing a statue even if it was so old?

'Well we're not here to talk about the statue. Let's get started, shall we? asked Dr Michal. However Zerach was intrigued and wanted to know more.

'How old do you think it might be?'

'Zerach, we need to start.'

'One quick answer Dr Michal and I'll be done. How's that?'

'Well if you must have an answer the man who gave it to me said it came from Israel. It was made during the Bronze Age, so as I said, it's very ancient.'

'But,' interrupted Benjamin, I always thought that the stuff that came from the Bronze Age wasn't very sophisticated. This looks so perfect it seems impossible.'

'Well who knows? Benjamin. I'm taking the word of a very old friend of mine. For all I know it could be a fraud. But enough, we must get started. As you know, Zerach and I have had three sessions and it's as I thought. He has the classic symptoms of schizophrenia. Fortunately there are drugs that are very effective in treating it. We now use second generation antipsychotics that control the symptoms that Zerach has. I've decided to start with a Drug called Zyprexa.'

She waited for them to speak but as they said nothing she continued. 'I know this may sound daunting, but we can help Zerach. His delusions may worsen over time if he doesn't start on the medication as soon as possible.' She waited again but the silence said it all.

Zerach felt sorry for his parents but not for himself. He had no intention of taking anything. Nothing and no-one would deprive him of the task he must complete. He was not unwell. He did not need to be fixed. He was not broken even though the psychiatric assessment said he was. He was he knew, a perfectly sane boy who was experiencing something special. **His** specialness was not the result of an illness. It was his Gift.

They had left and returned home. His mother, he knew was trying to stop herself from crying and he could see that his father was not happy with the suggested medical treatments. He pretended to take the medication and continued to attend family therapy. He never mentioned the voices that he heard every night. He was learning how to deceive and he was surprised at how easy it was becoming.

CHAPTER FIVE

Zerach had to find a way to stop talking in his sleep. He had made a mistake **one that** could potentially **put his mission at risk.** He wondered if he can ask the voices to stop him talking when he was Dreaming of them. Surely, if they indeed they were supernatural beings they'd have the power to do such a small thing.

He knew after what had happened that his dad would be listening for the slightest sound he might make after he went to bed. He would stand, like an ancient Roman Praetorian guard protecting his son from danger.

He walked to his mirror. It needs to be moved. It's placed exactly where the sun will strike it at dawn and needs to be synchronised with the changing seasons. He is fanatical about not letting anyone touch it. His mother had moved it once and they'd argued. She'd left hurt and confused, but he knew that it must only be moved by him. He cleaned it each day with a special micro fibre cloth he had purchased.

The twelve signs of the zodiac were harder to keep clean. He now used a tooth brush and a natural soap to keep them looking new. They were not. He knew that the mirror was very old. The fact that it had survived for so long with its original mirror and gilding was remarkable.

One morning, a year after he had the mirror in his room, he wanted to know more about it. He'd waited for both of his parents to be out and had placed it in a large suitcase after having carefully wrapped in several layers of clothes.

He had never been into an antique shop before. He stood outside of the shop for a moment and suddenly felt reluctant to go in. What if the mirror was not as old as he thought? What if it turned out to be a cheap mass-produced mirror made in China and sold **but** thousands to ordinary people in their suburban homes? It would render it useless. It would simply be a bauble made to attract the buyer who wanted to add something of mild interest to show to guests. He turned away and had gone a few metres when he heard a man call.

'Hey lad. What have you got there? I was watching you from inside of my shop. You looked like you were carrying the Crown Jewels. I half expected to see a London bobby arrest you.'

Zerach looked back. He saw a small, pixie like man who was Dressed in an old fashioned double-breasted suit. A pocket watch hung from a golden loop and he wore a hat which was reminiscent of a previous era. Intrigued he started to walk back.

'Bring it in young sir. I can hardly talk to a mirror without you showing it to me, now can I?'

For a moment Zerach was too shocked to speak. How could the man know that he was carrying a mirror in his suit case? He felt a moment of fear but the man took him by his arm and gently led him into the shop. Zerach looked around. The room was crammed with antiquities. There were old tomes, paintings, furniture, bric-a-brac dozens of glass fronted cabinets where the expensive pieces were displayed.

'This is the smallest of the rooms. I've another three. I don't know where it all comes from. I know I go to auctions but half of the stuff I don't remember buying. I do remember the mirror that you have in your case.'

'How can you possibly know that I'm carrying a mirror? It was a guess wasn't it?' Zerach knew he sounded foolish. Guessing the contents of an unopened suit case would defy the mathematical odds of this happening. This was not, he knew instinctively, a random coincidence.

'I can see you're confused. So was I when I was picked. Thought I was going crazy. They sent me to a hospital. I was told I was mentally unwell. I was stupid enough to believe them. I took their bloody medication for a few years and stopped.'

Zerach was too surprised to speak. 'You're confused. It's only natural. You've been told that you were ill and you're not. It's important for you to know that there are people who are genuinely unwell and a psychiatrist can help. Occasionally, however, people like you and a few others are not delusional. What we see and hear is real. So, sit yourself down for a moment and I'll make up a nice cup of tea. Not with those silly tea bags but proper brewed tea.' Zerach wanted to tell him he didn't really like tea but if it meant having some answers he was almost prepared to drink anything.

As he waited he looked more carefully around the room. There were suits of armour, old military helmets, masks, bottles of strange colours **and** medieval tapestries all jumbled together as if in a child's play room.

He got up and took a closer look at the amour. He knew that it couldn't be from the Middle Ages but it looked so authentic. It had dents in it and didn't look at all like the armour he had seen in movies when the knights were jousting. They lacked sophistication and he knew that they weighed a great deal. He looked at the tapestry that hung near the small shop window. He saw the faded threads that formed a hunting scene reminiscent of what he had seen in museums when he and his parents had gone to France and saw the famous Bayeux Tapestry.

He had been astonished **at** its size. He could still remember it as it stretched along the wall for seventy metres showing the events that led up to the Norman Conquest. This one, of course, was not the Bayeux Tapestry. That was over nine hundred years old. There was no way that such a carpet of the same period could be in this strange shop in Adelaide. He peered at the stiches. As he focussed more intently he thought that he could make out three circles that seemed to be hovering over one of the knights in the tapestry. They were the same colours as the lights he had glimpsed the other night when he was in bed. He felt himself shiver.

How could coloured spheres which were identical to those that he's seen be in an old tapestry? He felt he was somehow inextricably linked to something that was both powerful and mystical. Part of him didn't want the gift but he knew that he'd been chosen.

Reuben returned unsteadily carrying a tray that contained a large tea pot covered in a tea cosy. There were dainty porcelain cups that sat next to the tea pot and a small plate was covered in tiny iced cakes.

'You can't refuse an invitation to having a nice cup of tea and some cupcakes. I made them this morning with the passionfruit icing that you like so much.' He put the tray down and gestured for Zerach to sit. Zerach sat. How could this man know so much about him? It was impossible.

'One sugar and not too much milk I think. Does that sound about right?' Zerach nodded and his sense of unease grew. This man seemed to know everything about him. Even how he preferred to have his tea when he had to drink it to keep his old aunties happy when he went to visit them.

He stirred in his sugar and waited. 'Don't wait for me lad. Grab a cake. They'll be grand.' Zerach dutifully picked up one of the cakes. It had yellow icing and lots of passion fruit on it. 'Go on take a big bite. We're not dining with the queen you know. There's just me and you all cosy and snug in our little retreat.' Zerach felt as if he had tumbled into an Alice in Wonderland world full of the inexplicable. 'Finish up your cake and I'll answer your questions. I know that you feel scared. It's understandable. Your world is changing and you are changing as well. All change involves fear. It's how we grow. Now,' he added after he had drained his second cup of tea, 'ask away.' Zerach had no idea where to start. There were so many questions. What should he ask first?

'Don't worry about the order of the questions. This isn't one of those silly television programmes. Just start.'

'How do you know so much about me? I've never met you before and you know what cakes I like and how I take my tea. You know about the voices and how the psychiatrist said I'm ill. You can't know these things! It's not possible.'

'Zerach, take a deep breath and I'll get to the answers. We need to take our time so that you understand. Try not to be frightened. It's hard for you but you are the first of The Chosen. There hasn't been a Chosen one for many centuries.'

'But **how** can you know that? You're a stranger man who makes me tea and bring out little cakes. And now you're calling me by my name. I've never met you. How can you possibly know my name?'

'I've used your name and I **haven't** told you mine. I should have introduced myself. My name is Reuben. Rueben Goldberg. As you can see I'm old, far older than you can imagine. As you learn more I will tell you more about myself but you're not ready yet. I've run this little antique shop for many years. I don't make much money but I can afford to make special cakes for a special guest. What else can I tell you about me? I have a cat who's called Kenin. It's Yiddish but enough of me and my cat. Let's get down to your questions. Where do you want to start?'

'You know my name. You know about the voices. You know about me and the others who are supposed to be chosen. You also you know about the spheres. Someone must have told you. You can't just guess stuff like this. Can you please tell me how you know so much?'

'That's covered pretty much everything I think Master Zerach. This is going to be a little hard to believe but I promise you that everything that I'm saying is the truth. I will never lie to you. In fact, I'm forbidden to lie to you.'

'Forbidden? Who can forbid you? You said you were going to tell me the truth and you're being evasive.'

'Zerach,' said Reuben as he lent forward and touched Zerach's arm. 'I am forbidden. You must let me finish what I have to say and why you found me.'

'I didn't find you. I wasn't looking for you,' Zerach said.

'But I was looking, or to be more precise waiting for you. I've been waiting for you for many, many years. If I told you how long you wouldn't believe me. Let's just say it's been far longer than you can imagine. I know this is hard for you. We've tried so many times and have never really succeeded. We got close once and then . . . well you don't need to know that bit, but now we've found you. Zerach you have no idea how special you are. You were born special and you started to have your first Dreams about the other three Chosen ones when you were four. Isn't that right?'

'How can you know my Dreams? You can't know my Dreams. No-one can. It's not possible.'

'Zerach I know it sounds like it's impossible but obviously it isn't. Am I right in saying you've known of the other three since you were four years old?'

Zerach hesitated. He wanted to flee. To escape this man who knew too much. He'd never felt so vulnerable and exposed. It was as if his life were being played out in some insane way to a man he'd never met before. He tried to think of an explanation. A few moments later he said: 'This isn't real. I've had a relapse. You seem real to me but you're not. It's my illness. It's come back and I'm hallucinating.

'This is real Zerach. It's not a reoccurrence of your illness because both of us know that you weren't ill. Don't we?' he asked gently.

For the first time ever, Zerach wished he was sick. That he did in fact have schizophrenia. But he knew that he wasn't and never had been. He looked at Reuben's eyes trying to read what they might be saying. He saw that Reuben's deep brown eyes were full of compassion. He looked at Zerach as if he were his father. He saw gentleness, love and compassion. This man whatever or whoever he was meant him no harm.

Reuben smiled, stood up and put his arm around Zerach's shoulder. He felt its strength. It was a strength that Zerach somehow knew was a physical strength and something far more. His eyes had radiance that reminded Zerach of the rays of the sun that hit his mirror in the morning. Could he trust him? He looked for a moment longer and made up his mind. He wiped his eyes and tried to smile.

'A little smile. That's a good start. An excellent start in fact. You will need to listen carefully and try not to use your rational mind. That rationality comes from your brain, but you need to listen with your soul. I know you don't speak Yiddish but here's a little saying you might like to remember. "Yashir koyech." It means may your strength increase. You're going to need all of your strength to achieve your goal. Firstly you need to find the other three who are The Chosen. You've seen them in your Dreams. Soon the spheres will tell you their names. I will see you again when you need me. Go now Chosen One.'

Rueben went to shake Zerach's hand but to Zerach's surprise he found himself hugging him. He felt again his goodness and his love. 'Yashir koyech Zerach.'

"Thank you. Do you know how long I'll have to wait for the spheres to give me the others their names?'

'No. Something's are beyond my knowledge. Wait and try to be patient.' Reuben smiled and opened the door and gave a small bow as Zerach left.

After Zerach closed the door Reuben felt his own fear. These were powerful creatures that were communicating with Zerach. Zerach would need great strength and courage. He hoped, unlike last time they would be successful. The last Chosen One's name was Zerach although his Aramaic name was said differently. But in the end the tasks were too much. It had destroyed him. He would not, he vowed, allow Zerach to fail, even if he had to die to save him.

CHAPTER SIX

Zerach left the shop and still feeling dazed he entered the rush of the busy street. Cars, buses, trucks and motor bikes all sounded cacophonous to him. Why he wondered didn't he notice how noisy the world was? He wanted to block out the sounds and felt the urge to put his fingers into his ears but knew he'd look like a fool walking down the street like that.

He pulled his mobile phone from his pocket and instead of playing from his favourites list he typed he shut his eyes and pressed. He had no idea what piece of music he would hear. Unbeknownst to him the music was Concerto for Flute and Harp. Its ethereal tones enchanted him and he could feel it caressing him as if he was a child. Although he did not know it the key was in C major but he could hear that it was in three movements. Three movements, he thought and three spheres. Was it a coincidence? He no longer knew how to distinguish the two. After the music finished he got up and with the music still in his mind he made his way home.

As he walked up the path that led to his house he realised that he had left his mirror at Reuben's shop. So much had happened he had forgotten his original purpose. He had failed to ask a single **question about the mirror.** He shook his head and decided that he would go back to Reuben's after school the next day.

He went inside and his Dad was busy in the kitchen and his mum was pretending to read as she **sat** on the couch. Their dog wagged its tail and ran in small circles around his feet. It had been a stray that they had rescued from the pound, and, although it looked like a cross between a sausage and a dish mop it had such a gentle nature, that as soon as they had seen it they knew that it was meant for them.

His mother looked exhausted. If he was The Chosen One, why did it have to cause his mother so much pain? Impulsively he went to the couch and sat next to **her** and rested his head gently on her shoulder. He could feel her pain and then her joy as he continued to lean on her shoulder. She reached out and took his hand. He saw the tears well in her eyes.

'Mum I'm fine. Just because I have nightmares sometimes and speak in my sleep doesn't mean that I'm getting sick again. Everyone has nightmares and lots of people speak in their sleep. It doesn't mean that their sick. Does it?'

'No. You're right. I'm sorry. I worry too much. You're taking your medication and going to school although', she added, 'you're not coming with us to the synagogue anymore. But, I suppose that's part of growing up. Sometimes we have to give something up only to find it again.' She patted his hand and gave him a smile.

He went outside and as he walked out into the garden he heard his father's voice. Although he couldn't hear what he was saying his tone was unmistakable. He sounded worried. He was talking in a mad rush as if time were so precious that not a moment could be lost.

Zerach went a little closer. He knew that he should have called out but he said nothing and crept closer. He could hear snatches of the conversation. 'Yes. A few nights . . . then I thought . . . No. I'm sure that . . . Yes, that's what I think.' His father abruptly stopped talking and clicked off his mobile phone.

'Zerach I didn't hear you. What are you sneaking about for?'

'I wasn't sneaking. I couldn't find you. How come you're hiding behind a tree?'

'Zerach I'm not hiding. I was just having a chat with a friend.'

'It didn't sound very friendly to me. You sounded worried. You've always taught me to tell the truth. So please Dad. Who were you really talking to?'

Benjamin hesitated and coughed. He looked at his son and Zerach could see the confusion in his face. 'I was going to tell you later but you have the right to know. I've made an extra appointment for you with Dr Michal.'

'You what?' Zerach asked. He couldn't believe that his father had made an extra appointment without talking to him first. 'Zerach I'm sorry. Sometimes when you're a parent you have to make hard decisions. I know I could have asked you but you would have said that you're fine. But you didn't sound fine when I heard you the other night. You sounded distressed and scared.'

'May I ask a question?'

'Zerach since when did you have to ask me that? Of course, you can.'

'Have you ever had any nightmares?' He saw his father hesitate and slowly he nodded his head. 'Yes, I have. I suppose most people do at some time in their lives.'

'So, it's normal?'

He saw that his father knew that he had been outmanoeuvred. 'It must be, I suppose, **he answered.'**

'But what you're saying is that because I had a nightmare therefore I'm delusional?'

'It's not that straight forward, Zerach. I can't risk it. If I'm wrong, Dr Michal can tell me.'

'I think that's unfair. I'm being put on trial because of a Dream?' Zerach glared at his father and started to walk away. 'Please Zerach stop. We can talk this through.'

'No Dad we can't. You've made the appointment. You've made your decision and I have no say at all.'

'You can say whatever you like to Dr Michal. That's what's she there for.'

'I know that. I've been seeing her every six weeks for ages. Now I have to listen to her again. All she does is keep asking me if I'm taking my medication. I always say that I am. She looks at me as if I'm some sort of specimen. That I'm just this kid who's a schizo and need to be medicated up to the gills to keep me under control. I hate going to see her.'

Each time he went she sat smiling from her chair and all the while she was assessing everything about him. The tone of his voice. The length of time it took him to answer her questions. The way she could read his body language.

Initially he had been ignorant of the depth of her skills. He knew that he had to convince her that he was fine **even** though he was lying about taking his medication. Going every six weeks was an ordeal that seemed to get harder, not easier. 'Why haven't you told me before?'

'Dad what difference would it have made? She's a friend of yours and as you've said she's the "expert." What choice do I have?' He saw the pain on his father's face, and as he was about to answer they heard the harsh cawing of crows. Zerach looked, trying to locate where they were.

Finally he saw them. Their yellow beaks opened and he saw their avian eyes staring at him. He stared back. As he did the birds started to frenetically peck on the tree's branch. The sound had a primitive rhythm that sent out a staccato noise that reverberated about Zerach and his father.

Somehow he knew that he had to avoid looking into the eyes of the birds. It felt as if he were being hypnotised. He tried to shut his eyes but their stares seemed to have him in their control. He felt as if he were caught in a nightmare. He tried to resist. His fear grew and he felt his panic rising. He started to shiver and the sweat poured down his face and arms.

Desperately he tried to think. Suddenly he saw a shimmer of light. First one. Then two. Then three. His three circles of light. They circled over the birds. The birds cowed down and gave one last raucous croak and flew off. The lights of the spheres faded. Then they were gone.

Zerach looked at his father. He looked shocked and his face was grey. 'I've never seen anything like that before,' he said. 'Never. It was if . . . as if they were deliberately . . . it was if they were trying to frighten us.' He looked at Zerach and went to him. 'Are you okay?' Zerach tried to disguise his fear and gave a weak smile.

They walked inside and his father went to the fridge and took out two soft Drinks. 'I could do with something a bit stronger but these will have to do.' He handed a Drink to Zerach and they sat down at the kitchen table. 'Can we forget about the birds please Dad? There's no way we can explain it anyway.'

'It's unnatural for crows to behave like that. Still you're right. It's over now and there's not much point in trying to work out what happened.' The only sound they could hear was the Dripping of the tap. As Zerach listened, he noticed that the Drips had started to take on the same rhythmic tapping as the birds. Had he really seen the three spheres? If so, how did they scare away the crows? Perhaps his dad was right. He was ill and was trying to deny it.

CHAPTER SEVEN

His father Drove Zerach to Dr Michal's. He was late. 'It's a bit after eight o' clock. I know that you don't want to see her but as I said earlier it's for the best.' He looked at his son but he was ignored as Zerach stared out of the windscreen feigning indifference. His father sighed and Zerach knew he wanted to say more but **his father** tightened his lips and started tapping on the steering wheel.

Too soon they had arrived and he went into the waiting room. The radio played its usual inane songs that he loathed. He pulled out his phone and selected favourites on his music list and plugged in his ear phones. He felt himself relax and he shut his eyes preparing himself to sound convincing in his session. Before the song ended Dr Michal came in, and as always shook his hand as if she were meeting him for the first time. He found it odd but was too polite to comment. He shook her hand and she as usual held his for longer than was necessary and smiled.

As usual there was something about her smile that he found disconcerting. She looked into his eyes as if seeking to enter his mind and all the while she kept smiling as if she were frozen in a photo saying "cheese" to the camera. Her smile mimed warmth but without success. He could never understand how his father could have been friends with her.

'Come on in Zerach. I've scheduled you in for a full hour so we have plenty of time to talk about your dad's concerns. I heard that you're having disturbing nightmares and saying strange things in your sleep. We thought it best to check with you to see how things were going.'

'It was just a stupid Dream. I don't understand why everyone's so bothered.' He refused to give her eye any contact and his foot tapped impatiently on the floor.

'Zerach I think that you feel that I'm being intrusive and that your dad's over reacting. If that's the case then we can move on and that will be the end of it. He may, or may not, be placing too much importance on the Dream. But he was distressed and he's not a man who gets distressed easily.'

As she waited Zerach continued to look down and saw he was still tapping his foot. He forced himself to stop. He knew how she would interpret his action. She would interpret it as a sign of agitation. Again, he felt the pressure of having to try to outwit a woman, who, though ostensibly on his side he was always uneasy. He knew that he was clever and he knew that her intelligence was superior to his own. He needed guile and the ability to convince her that a Dream was insignificant.

He heard the clock ticking and looked around the room and as he did he saw again the small painting that hung on the wall above the old-fashioned fire place. It was a sombre painting that he found mildly disturbing although he didn't really understand why.

Without saying anything he got up and stood looking at it. He saw a dark, swirling sky that was more purple than black. As he peered closer he saw something that sent a shiver down his spine. There were three small smudges. He strained his eyes to see better and then the shapes took on their form. They were birds, three of them. And he knew at once what they were.

The crows sat on a branch their yellow beaks giving out a dull gleam and their eyes had the same menace as those that he and his father had seen the day before. He felt his head spin and he fought to control himself. He knew it was vital that he seemed unperturbed though why he knew this he neither knew nor understood.

He wiped his forehead and forced himself to calmly walk back to his seat. He could feel her eyes on him and he knew that he must soon return her gaze for if he didn't he would, he knew, be seen as practising avoidance.

'It's interesting isn't it? she said. 'What made you look at it today Zerach?'

'I don't know really. I've never taken much notice of it and for some reason I thought I'd have a look. It's a bit morbid to have in your office. I thought that psychiatrist would have pleasant paintings to reassure their patients.'

'Yes, I suspect that most do. I just like it for some reason. If it troubles you I can take it down.'

'No, it's fine,' he lied.

'I see that you noticed the birds Zerach.'

'Yes. Why would someone want to paint a dead tree with tiny crows on the branches?'

'It's not my area of expertise Zerach. Lots of artists were not always in the best state of mind when they created their paintings. Look at poor Van Gogh's work. Brilliant but he was a schizophrenic like you and yet he created masterpieces.'

'I don't think that painting would ever be considered a masterpiece.'

'No. I suspect not. Tell me though Zerach why did you get distressed **when you saw the** crows?' You seemed as if you were afraid of them. Was that what you dreamt about?'

'No.'

'So, you know what you didn't' Dream about?'

He was, he knew trapped. He had made a mistake. By allowing her to know that he knew the Dream had nothing to do with birds then he must have some knowledge of what he dreamt. In spite of his efforts she had outwitted him in less than ten minutes.

'I don't know.'

'But you just said that you knew what it wasn't about. It has to follow that you remember at least a few fragments of the Dream.'

'Well I can't. I'm sorry but I can't pretend to remember something when I didn't.'

She looked at him and sat waiting. He could feel her exerting pressure on him to tell her what he saw. He knew that he mustn't mention the spheres. But she was fishing. But fishing for what exactly? It was if she knew somehow that he had experienced something extraordinary and she needed it confirmed.

'I think that you can Zerach. I think that you're deliberately keeping something back from me.'

'Why would I do that?'

'As I see it there are two possibilities. **The first is that** you think the dream might mean that you're having a relapse **or** that what you dreamt is trying to tell you something that you don't want to share with me.'

'I've never kept anything back from you before. Why should I start know?' He looked at her determined to hold her gaze and not look away.

'Zerach you need to stop pretending. I know what your Dream was.'

'But you can't! How can you possibly know? I think that you're the one who needs psychiatric help not me.'

'Tell me about the spheres Zerach. What did they say?'

'Spheres? What spheres?'

'Zerach the time of pretending is over.'

'You're starting to sound like some sort of mad witch. I'm the one whose supposed to have a mental illness not you.'

'I'm not mad Zerach. Not one bit.'

'But you didn't deny that you might be a witch.'

'I think you have the wrong idea of what a witch is. They were usually wise women who knew things that others didn't. Some of them may have had psychic abilities as do I. All you need to do is learn to trust me.'

'I do trust you,' he lied.

'We both know that's not true but if you want to get better you need me, and by me, I mean all of the skills and powers that I have.'

'I'm leaving. I'm telling dad that you're mad thinking that you have special powers.'

'No Zerach you won't. You may but **you won't** be able to. We're entwined.'

'Entwined? Entwined? Now I know there's something wrong with you. Don't expect me to come and see you anymore because I won't be. And don't try to stop me. No-one can.

'Unfortunately, Zerach there are two of us who can stop you. One is me and the other is . . .' She reached over and caressed the black angel. 'Him, Zerach, him. He's called The Lord of Light or The Lord of Darkness. He went by both names. His powers are far, far greater than you can imagine. But you will meet him later. You won't be disappointed. It won't be long now. Things are happening and you're at the centre of it. You have to come to me and to him. Together we can . . .'

He didn't wait for her to finish. He flung back his chair and ran.

CHAPTER EIGHT

He ran through the front office and dashed across the road. Cars tooted their horns and he heard the screech of brakes as a bus slewed sideways missing him by centimetres.

He continued to run oblivious as to where he was going. He had one purpose **which was** to escape from the madness of Dr Michal and what she seemed to be planning. In spite of the pains in his legs and his ragged breath he forced himself onward.

The trees on the street cast their shade onto the footpath, creating silhouettes that danced and waved at him as if each was trying to ensnare him. Shadows of branches seemed to take on the shape **of** long fingers which were intent on ensnaring him and dragging him into the darkness.

He thought of the statue its beauty and menace and of how the painting and its birds had the sense of malignancy that seemed more menacing as each tree tried to grab him and hold it in their darkness. He could feel his panic increasing and he cried out to a God in whom he no longer believed. A rainbow appeared above the trees and he stopped astonished by the coincidence. His fear abated somewhat and he stopped running.

He stopped outside a small shop. He needed to escape the silhouettes. He was, he knew in spite of the rainbow still in danger. Had the rainbow even been real? Did he conjure it up out of his mind to allay the fear that he felt would overwhelm him? Had he imagined the menace of the tree's shadows, or even worse, had he invented in his head the entire episode in Dr Michal's office? Could he really be ill after all? Trees **don't ensnare** anyone or anything let alone try to drag people into the darkness. He had to talk to **someone whom** he could trust.

He thought back to the antique shop and to Reuben whose kind face and deep-set eyes seemed to know so much and held so much love. He walked to a bus stop that would take him into the city. Once he was there he could walk to Reuben's shop and tell him everything.

He felt relieved that he had a plan and someone who would listen to him without making any judgments. He waited for a few minutes and to his surprise the bus pulled up and he punched in his ticket in the validating machine and sat at the front.

It was, as always frustratingly slow. It stopped at every bus stop and soon the bus was full of people all sitting in silence wrapped up in their own little bubbles of existence as they stared at their mobiles or looked listlessly out of the dusty windows.

At last he arrived. He quickly got off and started to walk to Reuben's shop. The cars seemed excessively loud as they rushed along the busy road. He could hear the loud and angry- sounding blast of car horns as they impatiently beeped at Drivers who were slowing them down.

He couldn't breathe. His heart started to race and he was beginning to feel detached from his body. He tried to ignore it, but the pains in his chest intensified. He struggled to get air into his lungs. He stopped and tried to slow down his breathing but it was impossible. Then, without warning, he saw himself as if he were in a movie. He saw a young man who looked desperate and ill. A person marooned amidst the crowd as they flowed past him. He felt faint and perspiration flooded down his body. Wave after wave of terror travelled through him. He wanted to flee. To escape this person who seemed to belong to someone else.

He felt a hand on his shoulder. Rueben, he thought. Somehow Reuben had found him. He was rescued. Relieved he turned and looked into the eyes of a young woman. 'Are you all right?' she asked.

He wanted to say he wasn't. That he needed help. Feeling ashamed he ignored her. He stumbled on. Finally he began to recognise shops with which he was familiar. He now had only a few hundred metres to go. He walked faster. Then, unable to stop himself, he broke into a run.

As Reuben's shop Drew closer he felt himself beginning to relax. Then, at last, he arrived. He smiled. He would be safe. He looked for the antique sign that was written on the bowed glass window of Reuben's shop. He looked again. Something was wrong. The window was not bowed. It was modern and gleamed in the sunlight. Rows of meat of all descriptions were artistically arranged amidst sprigs of parsley.

He stood back and checked that he was in the right spot. Reuben's shop sat between a Dry cleaner and a book shop. He walked the few metres back to the Dry cleaners and trying to ignore the meat display he went to the book shop. Both were where they had always been. Confused and alienated he walked into the butcher' shop. He waited as an elderly woman chose her few pieces of meat. They were expertly wrapped and she placed them in her bag and walking with the aid of her walking stick she slowly left the shop.

'I was wondering . . .' He couldn't finish his sentence. His mouth was Dry. He tried to move his tongue to encourage some saliva. He tried again. He didn't sound like him but he was beyond caring. 'I was looking for the antique shop. It's called Reuben's. I must have got my streets mixed up.'

'Reuben's? Never heard of it. I've been here for over twenty years and there's no Reuben's here. And to the best of my knowledge there's never been a Reuben's anywhere around here. Are you sure that you're not lost?'

'But I was there the other day. I spoke to him. He's an old Jewish man and he sells antiques.'

'I'm sorry mate but I can't help you. I think you need to retrace your steps and see if you can get your bearings.' The doorbell jangled as a customer came in and stood waiting to be served. 'Good luck mate,' the man called as Zerach left. He started to wrap up the customer's order when he stopped and called to Zerach as he was leaving. 'The woman who was here before you. She's lived in this area all of her life. She's nearly ninety but still as sharp as a tack. If you hurry you might be able to catch up to her. She may be able to help.'

Zerach nodded and ran down the street. He hoped that being old she wouldn't be too far in front of him. He pushed his way through the crowd. Suddenly he saw her. She walked slowly, pulling her shopping cart behind her. She stopped at the intersection and pushed the button to cross the road. Zerach ran to her and tapped her on her shoulder.

'Excuse me. I was wondering if you could help me please. **I'm** looking for **Reuben's** antique shop.'

'Reuben? Reuben? I don't understand son. Reuben's shop hasn't been here for over eighty years or even a bit more. I used to go there with my mother. She loved antiques. But I was only a young girl. You're eighty years too late.'

'But he was there a few days ago. There must be some mistake.'

'There's no mistake. I may be old but my memory is perfect. Besides, he died long ago. Is this a prank of some sort? You're not trying to play silly buggers with me, are you?'

Zerach didn't hear her. The world had darkened and he felt himself fall into the blackness.

CHAPTER NINE

He heard muffled voices. There were two of them. One was the voice of a man and the other a woman. He couldn't understand what they were saying. He kept his eyes **closed** not wanting to find out what was happening. He felt something. An instrument of some sort was briefly placed on his ear.

'His temperature is quite high. He's got a fever of some sort.'

'His heart is okay. The ECG is fine. His pulse is rapid but regular. We should be there soon.' He could feel the movement of the ambulance as it made its way down the noisy streets. He thought back to what had happened. He tried to make sense of it, but how could he explain the impossible? There was no explanation for the disappearance of Reuben's shop. Not only was the shop not there, but Reuben, the man on whom he was going to rely, had died eighty years ago. He heard himself moan. He became agitated and tried to sit up. A hand eased him back down on the stretcher. He struggled but was too weak to resist.

'You're going to be alright', said one of the **paramedics**.' You may have had a seizure, or perhaps it was a simple fainting episode. Try to relax. We'll be at the hospital soon. Your vital signs are quite good and you'll be able to go to the new Adelaide Hospital.' She took his hand and he felt her gentle sense of reassurance. 'Not long now. You're doing fine. When we arrive, you'll be taken to emergency department. It's simply a precaution. Once we're there the doctors will decide what to do. Close your eyes if you want to.' He did as he was told and soon the ambulance came to a stop.

'There's a bit of a wait. They haven't quite got rid of some of the teething problems at the new hospital. Try to be patient. If you feel sick let us know.' She gave his hand a squeeze and then to his surprise he fell asleep.

'Time to wake up young man. We're taking you to admissions. We've been kept waiting for twenty **minutes** but at last they're ready for us. The two medics drove into the admission parking area and soon Zerach felt himself being wheeled into the hospital. He felt the coolness of the air conditioner as they went forward. He watched the ceiling above him slide by and he heard the hum of voices around him.

'Bay three,' someone said. As he lay there he wondered if anyone had told his parents where he was. He reached for his mobile phone but it wasn't there making him feel alone and isolated from the outside world. He watched the clock as it measured out the time. Surely, he thought, someone must come soon. The lights seemed too bright, and the longer he lay there the more anxious he felt. Still, no one came. Another twenty minutes passed. He started to feel thirsty and needed to go to the toilet. He tried sitting up, but as he did, the room spun around him and he collapsed back onto the bed. Finally, he heard footsteps and a nurse came into the room.

'Sorry about the wait. It's absolutely mad in here today. Half of Adelaide seems to have the flu and the hospital is struggling to cope. Still, that's not your problem is it? I'll take your blood pressure and temperature. I see that you've had an ECG and that looks okay. The registrar shouldn't be too long. Try to get some rest if you can.'

'I need to go to the toilet,' Zerach said. 'Can I go to the bathroom?'

'Sorry mate. You'll have to use the bottle. Do you think you can manage by yourself?' Zerach nodded. He hated the idea but knew that he had no choice. The nurse came back with the bottle and Zerach tried to relax but it was impossible.

'Take your time. I'll come back in a few minutes. Everyone finds it a bit hard but you'll be fine. If you can't go we'll get a wheel chair and take you to the toilet. Whatever you do don't get up okay?'

Zerach gave a feeble nod and in spite of the nurses' instructions to relax he found it impossible. After a few minutes he grew annoyed and decided that he couldn't wait. He would find the bathroom himself.

He eased himself out of bed and gingerly sat on its side as he waited for the room to stop spinning. Finally, it stopped. He put his feet on the floor and cautiously waited, then slowly stood up. Again, the room span. He held his breath and tried to focus. Gradually he felt somewhat better. He took one step. Then another. He had gone a few more steps when he saw a doctor approaching. 'What on earth are you doing out of bed? You could have another episode.'

'Episode?'

'Yes. That's what I said.'

'But I just fainted, didn't I?'

'Look let's concentrate on getting you back to where you should be. You're going to be transferred to your ward. A doctor will see you as soon as possible.'

'But aren't you a doctor?

'Of medicine yes. But psychiatry isn't my area.'

'Psychiatry? What do you mean? I don't need a psychiatrist just because I fainted.'

'I'm afraid that is appears to be more serious than that.'

'I'm not going to see a psychiatrist! I see my own psychiatrist. I'm already being treated.'

'It's out of my hands I'm afraid. Come on. Let's get you transferred.'

He tried to run. He had taken a few steps when he crumpled to the floor. She summoned two orderlies and he was lifted onto a bed and wheeled away. He struggled to free himself but knew that he was too weak to escape.

'Come on lad,' said one of the orderlies. 'They'll get you sorted out.' He tried to free himself but he was gently restrained. As he moved along in his bed he saw a large blue sign that read 'Psychiatric Ward'. Under the sign was a painting. It was a replica of the painting in Dr Michal's office.

CHAPTER TEN

Dr Hannah Weinstock saw a boy being wheeled into the ward. She was the senior psychiatrist and was as usual tried and overworked. The rostering system seemed to have become more dysfunctional every day and she was looking forward to finishing work in a half an hour.

She checked her list. Three more patients to see. One had severe depression, another a borderline personality disorder and the last was crippled with anxiety and had attempted to take her own life. She sighed. Half an hour was not going to be enough to deal properly with these three patients. Once again, she would be forced to work overtime along with her colleagues who like her were becoming increasingly stressed.

She could hear his screams and she flinched. Although a seasoned practitioner she had never learned the art of being able to detach herself from her patients. It was both a blessing and a curse. She could be more empathetic but on the other hand the emotional cost to her was becoming increasingly difficult.

She walked towards the boy who by now was thrashing about on his bed. He was begging to see a man called Reuben. She assumed that Reuben was a family member and wondered why the boy needed him so desperately. Fortunately he had his Driver's licence so they knew his name and his parents had been called.

As she came closer she was shocked at how similar he looked like her son Thomas. He had the same, near perfect features and the same coloured hair and eyes. It was, she knew, a resemblance that she needed to ignore.

'We'll need to sedate him. I'm worried that he may hurt himself. Bring him in.' They wheeled him into a single bed room. He kept screaming out for Reuben. Suddenly he stopped 'The spheres. The spheres. They're back. Their calling for me.' He stretched out his arms and gazed upwards. It was as if he was viewing the cosmos and was at one with what he saw.

CHAPTER ELEVEN

'Let's get him settled,' said Dr Weinstock. She heard the quaver in her voice and saw a nurse approaching who had overheard her. 'Do we know who he is?' she asked above the continual cries that Zerach was making. 'Yes. By chance I happen to know his psychiatrist. I've rang her. She diagnosed his condition as schizophrenia and is treating him with Zyprexa. I think, in addition to a sedative, we'll increase the Zyprexa. Fortunately, Dr Michal has agreed. **The nurse** injected the sedative and within minutes Zerach started to calm down. 'I've given him ten milligrams of Diazepam. If he needs more I'll increase it to fifteen. I'll write up my notes.'

When she had finished she stood next to him staring down at his face. 'It's amazing,' she said to the nurse. 'He looks exactly like my son Thomas. I got such a shock when I first saw him.'

The longer she looked at Zerach the harder it became for her to resists the urge to run her fingers through his hair. How could one boy, who was not related to her, look identical to her son? If he was dressed in Thomas' clothes she would struggle to tell them apart.

She scribbled her signature on the bottom of the notes and turned to leave. 'I've rang his parents. They should be here soon. They can see him of course but if he starts up again contact me on my mobile.'

Zerach opened his eyes and shut them again. The lights were too bright and he had a headache. He remembered his terror and how he had been screaming out **Reuben's** name and talking about the spheres. He was angry with himself for losing control. It was essential that he continued to deceive Dr Michal and his parents that he was taking his medication. What if they increased his dose of his anti-psychotic Drug? Would his parents now be super cautious and ensure that he swallowed his tablets instead of pretending to? Just as he asked himself this he heard his parents talking as they walked down the corridor and towards his room.

He tried to lift his head from the pillow but couldn't. He needed to be alert but he knew that he had been given a Drug that caused him to feel sleepy. He tried to fight its effects but it was impossible.

It was then that his door opened. His parents came in and his mother was wiping her eyes with a tissue. He forced a smile and held out his arms. His mother rushed to him and hugged him. She took his face in her hands and lent forward and kissed him. He felt her tears on his face and saw the fear and confusion in her eyes. His father waited and when his mother got up he sat on the bed and held his hand.

'Thank God you're safe. The school rang and said that you hadn't arrived. We waited for what seemed like an eternity trying to think of where you might have gone. Finally, we received the call from the hospital telling us that you were here.'

His mother smiled and seemed unsure as to what to say. She sat down on the other side of the bed and stroked his arm. It reminded Zerach of when he was a child. She would stroke his forehead and sing to him before he fell asleep. She had always made him feel safe. When he hurt himself, she would kiss the pain away.

'You gave us a bit of a scare mate,' his father said with a fake grin. 'How are you feeling?' Zerach didn't know how to answer. What could he say? How could he explain the turmoil and fear without sounding unwell? He couldn't tell them about Reuben or the missing shop or about the spheres. It was impossible. He cleared his throat and quickly made the only decision that he felt offered him some hope. 'A big groggy but honestly I don't feel too bad. I was told that I was saying things but that's over now.'

'That's great Zerach,' his father said, 'but it's a bit more serious than that. I'm not sure if you're confused or have forgotten how you were behaving.' He waited for a moment and Zerach knew that his father was not going to be placated with lies.

'Dad I know I had some sort of seizure. I heard one of the nurses talking and that's what she said. I know that you're worried but I'll be home soon and then things will be fine again.'

'I wish it was that simple,' said his mother as she absentmindedly stroking his forehead. 'Unfortunately, it isn't. We spoke to Dr Michal and she is very concerned about what happened. She thinks you might benefit from a short stay in hospital.'

'Here? I'm not staying here! If I'm crazy like everybody thinks, including my own parents, what bloody difference does it make where I am? Hospital or home, I'm still a nut case according to the rest of the world.'

'Oh Zerach. Please don't say things like that. You have a mental illness. No-one uses labels like that anymore.'

'Tell that to the kids at school Mum. It was all supposed to be confidential but no. Word got around. All of the kids, **even my** dwindling list of friends are looking at me as if I'm going to attack them with a knife or an axe.'

He tried to stop his tears but as they flowed down his face he brushed them angrily aside.

'I wish I was a normal kid who could go to school, listen to music, got to the skate park and be treated like everybody else. But no. You both hover over me like I'm going to explode at any minute.'

'Zerach we have never stopped you from doing any of those things,' his father said. We've tried to keep an eye on you but what parent wouldn't?' He looked at Esther but she looked too distressed to speak. 'I'm not sure how I can Dress this up to make it sound less harsh. The truth is, however, that you did explode. You've had a severe psychotic episode. Pretending that everything's okay is simply not true. You're a smart young man. You know that what happened is serious and it can't be **ignored.'**

'What if . . . what if the so called experts are all wrong? What if you and the psychiatrists and all the stupid dick heads at school have got it wrong? What if I really am seeing and hearing things that are real?'

'Zerach I'm not a psychiatrist but I do know that you're not well. You hear voices. You speak to them in your Dreams. You think that spheres communicate with you. It's all a delusion. It's what people like you experience when they aren't well.'

'People like me? People like me? You're like the rest of them. Put me in my little mad box, shut the lid and then you can feel safe.'

'Safe?' His mother asked. 'What do you mean safe? From us?'

'From everyone. The teachers, the kids, the parents the whole stupid world. The world's mad, not me. Take a look around and see what's happening. You sit and watch the news every night and shake your heads but you just accept it. What's sane about what you see?'

'The world's in a mess but it always has been.'

'Dad are you saying because it's always been like that then it's normal?'

'I suppose. It's wrong. I wish it wasn't the way it is.'

'But what is normality? Aren't you really saying is that what the majority believes makes it sane or normal? And that anyone who doesn't fit in is insane?'

'Zerach that's a clever argument but it's flawed. I don't think there's much point in some kind of debate about the nature of reality. I'm a mathematician not a philosopher. If you need to talk more about this you need to take it up with Dr Michal.'

'No. I'm not seeing her again.'

'Zerach you have to. It will be part of your ongoing treatment after you've been stabilised in hospital. As your mother I'm not going to allow you to jeopardise your mental health.'

'And what about your mental health? Zerach asked.

'My mental health? Zerach I'm not the one in hospital. You are. You don't have to worry about me. You've got enough on your plate without worrying about me. My job is to love and nurture you. I have always loved you and always will. My so called mental health is irrelevant.'

'Is it? Then how come you have to take Valium?

'How do you know that? You weren't meant to know. You had enough to deal with without worrying about me. How long have you known?'

'I've known for ages. I also know that you take more than you're supposed to. I've seen the prescriptions from different doctor's surgeries. You're doctor shopping to get extra tablets.'

His mother turned away and went to the door but then turned around and without looking at Zerach she started to speak. 'I can see that you think that I'm being hypocritical in saying that you must take your tablets and that I take too many. I never wanted to tell you because I thought that it would make things harder for you but since you know I will.'

'I started having panic attacks after you were diagnosed. I'd had a few after you were born but haven't had any for years. Then when you got sick they started again. I was prescribed different Drugs but they made no difference so they put me on Valium.' She faltered then took a deep breath and continued. 'They seemed to work for a while but when I was told that you would probably have to stay on your medication for the rest of your life I blamed myself.'

'Why Mum? It wasn't your fault.'

'I know that rationally but no matter how hard I tried to tell myself I wasn't to blame I became fixated. I was having panic attacks nearly every day. Each day I had to stay strong for you. Then after about six months or so they seemed to be less effective but the doctor said how addictive they were and wouldn't increase my dose. So, I cheated. I managed to get more of them. Stole them in **fact.** I'm so sorry Zerach. Not much of an example, am **I?**' Zerach was about to answer but she pressed on. 'I feel ashamed. I'm so sorry Zerach.' Zerach slowly climbed out of his bed and went to his mother. 'I'm the one who should be sorry. None of this would have happened if it wasn't for me.'

He put his arms around her and then hugged her to him. He had never felt this close to her since he was a child. He had, he realised been too focussed on himself and hadn't, not for a moment, ever considered how he was making life difficult for his parents. Of course, he belatedly realised they would be worried and **possibly frantic.** Once again he wished that he had never heard the spheres and what they kept singing to him. Why couldn't he be a normal?

CHAPTER THIRTEEN

Zerach didn't eat meat. His dinner sat on a tray untouched as the black gravy made an island around a piece of steak. The fat in the meat had congealed after having sat for too long on his table and the vegetables looked as tired as he felt.

His parents had left promising to see him the next day but he wasn't sure he'd have the energy to deal with the new complexity of their relationship, especially now his mother was aware of Zerach's knowledge of her consumption of Valium.

As they had left he had heard his mother speaking in what she thought was a whisper to his father. Unfortunately, the acoustic of the room and the conjunction of the corridor enabled him to hear what she'd said.

'He's worse than I thought,' she'd said. He heard the anguish in her voice and could hear his father who was urging her to speak more quietly. He crept out of his bed and stood behind the open door of his room listening.

'I'm sure that he'll get all of the attention and treatment that he needs. He may not like being here but we have no choice. It's for the best. Perhaps they can get him to understand that he has a serious mental illness. It might sound odd but even though he's been seeing Dr Michal for so long I don't think he really understands that he's ill.'

'I'm sure that Dr Michal can get him sorted,' his father said as their footsteps echoed down the corridor.

***

Dr Michal smiled and reached for her mobile. It had taken all of her skills but she had done it. The boy was hers. Her plan had been to increase Zerach's medication incrementally as he visited her each week. She needed to be cautious. The boy's father, whom she knew well, had the reputation of being something of a mathematical genius at university. Whilst he would have little knowledge of pharmacology he would be suspicious if his son was placed very high dosage rates. Even though she knew he would trust her judgment she had to be cautious. In any event, any fool could use the internet and, in a few seconds, find out what the normal dose would be and how it was triated upwards. Benjamin was no fool, nor was his mother who was far sharper than most people realised.

Many years ago she had orchestrated an accidental meeting with Benjamin when they'd at university. She had watched him for some time. She knew that he used the computers in the library and he usually sat at the same one each day at eleven. It was obviously between his tutorials and she had deliberately positioned herself next to where he sat.

He had arrived a few minutes early and for a moment she thought he was going to change his mind as he was lost in conversation with his girlfriend who seemed annoyed. Eventually however, he had given the young woman a kiss and had sat down next to Michal. He sighed and logged on. She waited. After ten minutes or so she had turned to him and gave him her brightest smile. She knew that she was attractive. Had she not been she would not have been chosen but her looks along with her powers were a combination that she knew that he'd not be able to resist.

She sighed and then slapped the top of her work bench. She could remember almost verbatim what she had said at that first crucial meeting. 'Damn thing. It keeps freezing up on me and I'm losing my data. I backed it up but now the bloody things not been saved.' He looked at her and smiled back. She almost felt sorry for him. He was kind and courteous but she knew that she mustn't allow her emotions to stop what needed to be done. He would, unbeknownst to him, be the father of a boy who would have extraordinary powers. If this future child, who had already been conceived, was allowed to achieve his gift, then centuries of endeavour would be lost. He was the most powerful adversary that they had ever encountered. It was vital that he was stopped from achieving his psychic potential.

They had defeated so many. The last one had been powerful but, he had, like all of those before him been defeated. She knew that she and her kind were close to achieving what they'd striven for. Ordinary humans were easily manipulated. Inevitably their hubris or lust for power would enable her and her allies to create another scenario that would set up the string of events that led to war, famine, **and ultimately to total mayhem.**

The mass media had been their ignorant puppets who had broadcast the atrocities that now occurred daily. She and her group had thought that the First World War would cause enough horror which in turn would lead to a collective sense of loss of faith – that mankind would be forever at war in an endless cycle of terror and mayhem. They could then capitalise on this and The Lord of Darkness would descent. Alas they had been disappointed when their hoped for outcome had not eventuated.

The Second World War had been more promising. Its massive carnage and destruction had left millions dead and nations had had their national psyches destroyed. Times such as this bred despair and it was on despair that they fed creating the atmosphere that they would use and change the world forever.

Their group, under guidance from The Lord of Darkness, had infiltrated the Dreams of scientists and had implanted the knowledge of nuclear fusion. They had rejoiced at witnessing the unimaginable ravages of Hiroshima and Nagasaki. They had been so close. Hitler had been on the cusp of making a nuclear bomb but for reasons they couldn't understand had not managed to achieve what they had shown to his scientists.

Again, they tried. The Cold War and the Bay of Pigs had been the closest that they had come to victory. They were jubilant as the world waited for its first ever nuclear war. The two greatest and most powerful countries to have ever existed were within a few hours of nuclear attack. Chaos was what they craved. A return to the beginning of time, when chaos, as the ancient Greeks had known was the very first thing to exist. This time only the Darkness would emerge from the chaos, light would be banished and with it all hope and love that humans needed to survive as a species.

She knew what lay in the future, but there were variables over which they had no control. They had the ability to create fear, chaos and disasters but they were not gods. They could be stopped but only by someone who was stronger than their collective powers and his name was Zerach. She had to succeed.

She pulled her mind back. She had been careless. Thinking about the future was futile and had the potential to weaken what she must do. She smiled again at Benjamin and stood up feigning helplessness and uncertainty. He had looked at her and smiled back. 'Having troubles?'

'Stupid thing keeps freezing then losing my data. I'm supposed to be at a lecture but I'm a bit behind. I keep telling myself that I'll keep up with all of the work but sometimes it feels impossible.'

'We've all been there. It's a lot of pressure but I suppose when ones doing post grad work it's the nature of the beast.' She had to suppress her surprise at his use of the word 'beast'. It was an irony that nearly threw her but she forced herself to play her role of an earnest but pressured student. 'Can I give you a hand?'

'Could you? I don't want to intrude on your time.'

'No problem. Now let's have a look.' He cleared his throat and started going through a series of checks. A few minutes later he gave a thumbs up sign. 'Fixed the little gremlins. That should be fine now.'

'So soon? Don't tell me you're one of those computer geniuses that find this sort of thing child's play?' He looked embarrassed. She knew that she had to keep him talking so that she could create a nascent friendship that she could use to her advantage.

'I think I owe you a coffee. Can I get you one?'

'Really there's no need.'

'Please I'd like to. I'll grab a takeaway. Now let me guess. Flat white, skimmed milk and no sugar.'

'How on earth did you know that? he said.'

'Lucky guess.'

'Guessing is not my strength. Guessing in maths is frowned upon to say the least. On the other hand, the intuitive leap that produces the light bulb moment, well, that's considered genius.'

'So, Mr Genius will you let me get you your coffee?' He hesitated but she could tell that he was flattered and pleased.

'That would be great. Thank you.'

She went to the small canteen and lined up behind the few students, who as always stood as if they were in a trance trying to decide what to buy. Finally, she put in her order and took the coffees back and placed Benjamin's in front of him.

'Enjoy,' she said. She sat down and accessed the latest research papers that dealt with adolescent mental illness. She would specialise in this field for one reason only. It had to be her that oversaw Zerach's treatment some sixteen years into the future. It was essential that she established a reputation as the person who would be regarded as the best child psychiatrist who specialised in schizophrenia.

Gradually she had nurtured their friendship. Though they belonged to different faculties and didn't share the same building she ensured that their paths would cross. Each time she gave him her special smile and expressed her delight in their meetings. She met him for coffee and occasionally for lunch and after a few months she had suggested that they could meet for lunch each fortnight.

One day, over lunch Benjamin was particularly excited. He kept smiling as his foot tapped madly against the table. 'You look like you've got something to tell me. I've never seen you looking so happy'

'I'm not supposed to say anything yet but I have to tell someone. Since you're one of the few real friends I have at university I want to tell you first.'

'Well spit it our Benjamin. If you keep hitting the table with your foot for much longer I'll be diagnosing you with ADHD.'

'Guess what?'

'Benjamin I'm no psychic I'm hopeless at guessing. Tell me. I'm busting to know.'

'It's Esther. She's pregnant!'

'That's wonderful. Congratulations. How many months pregnant is she?'

'Nearly five. Just think Michal. I'm going to be a Dad.'

'And a great Dad you'll be. I'm quite sure of that. We should be Drinking champagne.'

'At midday?'

'No perhaps not. Still it's wonderful news'

'Isn't It?' He beamed and she leant over and gave him a hug. Have you chosen a name as yet?'

'Yes, but you'll have to wait.'

Several months later she had met Esther who was nearly full term. They had agreed to meet at a small cafe that was close to the university and Esther had walked in, a galleon of awkward grace as she carefully crossed the rough wooden floor of the cafe. Benjamin held her arm and they looked almost beatific in their joy. Michal had found it hard to manufacture enthusiasm and to behave as if she were pleased. She had noticed that as their child grew, her own powers diminished. It was minute diminution, but it was one she had not experienced before. Nevertheless, Michal smiled and gave Esther a brief peck on her cheek. 'Not long to go now. You must be so excited.'

'Thanks. Yes, I am but I'll be glad when he's born. I'm finding it harder every day.'

'So, the little one is a he then?' Michal asked.

'Yes. I wasn't supposed to say, but since I'm due so soon it doesn't matter.'

'Have you decided on his name?'

'Yes, and since you're such a good friend of Benjamin's I thought that you should be the first non- family member to be told.'

'Really? Thank you. So, don't keep me waiting. What is it?'

'Zerach,' Esther said. We both agreed ages ago that his name was going to be. We never had any doubts.' Michal smiled. She had never had any doubts either but it gave her pleasure to see what she had foretold come to fruition.

Michal got up from her seat and gave Esther a hug. It took an enormous amount of will not to convey her hatred at the child but she had learnt the art of deceit over centuries. She could not betray her feelings, no matter how great a threat that the child posed.

As she hugged Esther she felt Esther stiffen and Draw back. Alarmed, she checked to see that she had played her role convincingly. She let go but knew that she had not done anything wrong. Could Esther have sensed something?

'I'm sorry Esther. That must have seemed rude.' Esther gave a feeble smile and cleared her throat. 'I felt Zerach kicking like crazy. It was as if he . . .' she faltered and after a moment spoke. 'I suddenly felt vulnerable. It was if Zerach was somehow in danger. I'm being ridiculous. You'll be thinking that I'm just the sort of future patient you'll be seeing when you qualify as a psychiatrist. It must be my hormones playing up. He's never kicked so much before.'

'Perhaps he's had enough of being cooped up. He must think it's time for him to come out.' Esther had smiled but it was clear that Esther still felt uncomfortable and the lunch had finished early.

Michal had to be patient. If they intervened too early they risked the possibility they may not be able to learn the whereabouts of the other three. All of them needed to be destroyed.

When the time was ripe she knew that her tactics had been successful. She had of course known that they would be, but it was always rewarding when one's skills came to fruition.

Her plan and that of her group had been simple. Once the boy came to her she would make the diagnosis and prescribe Zyprexa. She had known that the recommended dose would not be able to stop his abilities. He would need larger dosages of the anti-psychotic combined with a sedative to prevent him from activating his gift. Her master never accepted failure.

CHAPTER FOURTEEN

Thomas

Thomas sat on his bed looking out of his small window. He held an old book in his hand and with the aid of a magnifying glass was once again trying to decipher the tiny writing that was written on the margins of the book. After several years of trying to understand what they represented he was becoming increasingly frustrated and disillusioned.

He had convinced himself that the symbols were runes which, if he could decipher them, would lead him to a secret discovery he could present to his parents. Both were in the medical field and as such, their scientific views did not sit with what he thought he'd found.

He had discovered it three years ago in the attic of their house. He could still remember the day he had rushed into the lounge room carrying the book as it were a scared talisman.

'Look what I found,' he'd said to his father. His father had looked up briefly from his laptop and glanced at the book. 'It must be something special. You look like you've won the lottery.'

Thomas had sat next to him and opened the book and showed the symbols to his father. 'Looks like a bird fell into the inkwell and went for a walk on the pages.' He handed it back to Thomas and added with a grin: 'Perhaps you've discovered a secret map to a treasure that's been buried in the garden. God knows, with the money its costing us to keep this mausoleum going is getting ridiculous.'

Thomas looked at his mother who was reading a crime novel. As a psychiatrist she enjoyed finding out the mistakes that the authors made and took a wry sense of pleasure when she found them. In spite of her desire to find mistakes she had felt embarrassed to tell her husband or son that she actually enjoyed reading them. She smiled back at Thomas and shook her head. Thomas knew that she wanted him to Drop the subject. Each time it was mentioned she had to placate her husband Daniel, who would fume and fuss as if they were paupers about to be thrown into the streets. Thomas looked at his father and waited. He didn't need to wait long before his father sighed and put down the research paper he was reading.

'Did you hear what I said Thomas?'

'Yes, Dad but I know that you and Mum love living here and you'll never move. It's our 'ancestral home. When I was little I actually thought that we lived in England and you were a Lord.'

'Really? Well your grandfather did have a title of some sort but he thought hereditary titles were a bit silly in Australia. Obviously, he was rich. Just look at the house he built. It cost a fortune and then after the depression he lost a great deal of money. Somehow, he managed to hang onto the house but all of the servants were dismissed except his butler. Not long after that he disappeared and my Dad was raised by his two aunties. Both of whom, I might add, were so eccentric that Dad's cousins wanted them put in the asylum.'

'What happened? And how come I was never told?' He leant forward eager to hear more about the family skeletons. 'I suppose it didn't seem that important and when you showed me the book I thought it was time to tell you.'

'There's more isn't there?' Thomas asked. He heard the excitement in his voice and held the book close to his chest as if it could reveal even more disclosures from his father.

'Daniel don't egg the boy on. The last thing he needs is more stories about our ancestors. From what I can gather half of them were shysters.'

'Grandad wasn't. It was pretty common for people of that era to have a different view on how they made their money. Besides, I don't want to get involved in a discussion about what is, or is not a crook as you so quaintly put it. I'm trying to tell our son a little bit of history. In any event,' he continued ignoring Hannah's sighs, 'if it weren't for them we wouldn't be living here. I'm never sure whether I should be pleased or not. Did I tell you how much the roof's going to cost to get fixed? He made a great deal of money and stupidly lost it.' He waited but Hannah said nothing but Thomas saw her smile as she put the book in front of her face.

'But what about the middle bits Dad? Why are you leaving them out? You said that your grandfather went missing. You can't just leave it there. How long was he missing for?'

'I wish now I'd kept my mouth shut but it's a fair question. He was never found. One day he was here apparently and then he wasn't.'

'But he must have gone somewhere?'

'The police had dogs looking for him and all of the neighbours were out looking for him as well. Finally, the dogs found a trace of his clothing but then they lost the scent.'

'Did they keep looking? If he was so wealthy and could have been a lord or something the police would keep looking.'

'The papers had a field day. I kept the paper for years. For all I know it might still be in the attic that is if the mice haven't eaten it.'

'Really? We have to find it Dad! We might be able to find a clue.'

'I think your mother is better at finding clues about people than I am.'

'Oh no you don't Daniel. I'm keeping out of this. If you want to go up to the attic and help Thomas that's fine. But I'm not going up there. I went once and it gave me the creeps.'

'I don't understand how you can find an attic creepy when you're a psychiatrist. Some of the clients that you've had have finished up in prison.'

'That's different. I trained for it. I didn't train for attic climbing. So no thank you. I hope you can find it. Daniel would find it interesting.

Go up with him and explore. It'll be a bonding experience between father and son.'

'You heard her Dad. That sounds like a challenge. A bonding exercise with a hormone ridden, sex mad adolescent.'

He laughed and his parents joined in. 'It's been a long time since we've all had a laugh. Go on **Daniel**. Off you go and don't forget the torches. Oh, and something to cover your face.'

'Why do we need to cover our faces?' Thomas asked sounding worried.

'Spiders. Hundreds and hundreds of them. Huntsmen, red backs, daddy long legs. A whole range of arachnoids waiting for you.'

'Mum! You know I hate spiders.'

'Every adventure has its price. Perhaps Daniel, it might be prudent to take the first aid kit with you.'

'I wasn't going **to** but after that I am. Come in Thomas let' go.'

'But the spiders Dad.'

'Yes, there may be the odd spider or two but it's not the horror chamber your mum's making it sound. She's teasing you.'

'Are you mum?'

'Yes, a bit. You'll be fine. Have fun.'

'Grab the torches Thomas. Our adventure is about to begin' He grinned at Thomas and soon they were climbing the old, wooden stairs to the attic.

'Welcome to the secret world of the spider kingdom,' Daniel said as he pulled down on the old light cord. The light flickered on for a moment then with a 'pop' it burst. They were surrounded by darkness and in spite of himself Thomas felt afraid. It wasn't only the spiders that worried him. There was something that he could sense but could not name. It felt both strange and familiar and he had no idea why.

'I'll go down and grab a couple of spare bulbs. Do you want to stay here or come with me? Thomas wanted to say that no, he did not want to say but thought his dad would think that he was being a chicken. 'No, he said,' trying to sound confident. He switched on his torch and its beam shimmered through the dust mites that danced in a hidden breeze somewhere in the attic.

'Are you sure?

'Yep. I'll be fine.' His dad went and he tried to make out what the attic contained. The torch was old and its beam feeble but he could make out shapes that were covered in layers of dust.

He tried to focus on what he could see rather than the flutter of claustrophobia that added to his challenge of staying there by himself. He took a few steps forward and stopped in front of one of the covered shapes. He reached out and as he was about to pull back the sheet when something flew at him. He ducked and he heard the flapping of wings a few metres above his head. He went to stand up when suddenly the bird attacked. He felt it pecking at his head and he yelled out in terror and confusion. The bird flew off and he sank to the floor. He had half risen when again it flew at him. He had managed to catch it in the beam of his torch. It was large and black and he felt it was trying to stop him from opening whatever it was in front of him.

He lay on the floor. The bird landed on his shoulder and let out a cry. It was a cry not of this world. It was alien and malicious. He felt its hatred and then once again it flew off and for a moment he thought it had gone.

He stood. It was a mistake. He felt the stabbing of its beak against his neck as if it knew that it was there that he was the most vulnerable. He tried to grab it but missed. This time it went for his eyes. Thomas screamed as he felt its frantic pecks. It had missed his eyes by a few centimetres. Again it plunged at him this time shrieking as it did. He struck out with his torch. It was too quick. Again, it tried but this time he was ready. He struck with his torch and felt a flush of pleasure as he felt the metal handle land somewhere on its body. Undeterred it tried again. Thomas swung the torch like a cricket bat and he felt the satisfying thud as it connected. It fell at his feet. He took the torch and **poked** at it. It lay still, its eyes staring at him and even though he was convinced that it was dead its coal black eyes still seemed to contain their malice.

CHAPTER FIFTEEN

'Everything okay in here? It sounded like you were practising your rap moves. What's all the noise?'

'It tried to kill me.'

'What?'

'The bird. It attacked me. It's bitten me on the head and tried to get at my eyes. It was as if it wanted to kill me.'

'Kill you? But how and why would a bird want to kill you. Are you sure that it wasn't simply frightened and got confused?'

'Dad it was trying to kill me. Look at the blood in my hair and my neck.'

'My God Thomas. Let's get you out of here.'

They slowly climbed down and stood on the landing. Thomas started shaking and fell to the ground. 'Hannah! Hannah! Come upstairs! It's Thomas. He's collapsed.' She threw the book to the floor and ran up the stairs.

'He said that a bird attacked him. I got him down and suddenly he just fell.'

'Thomas,' she said as she shook his shoulder to check if he was conscious. She waited for a moment and gently shook him. 'He's not responding. Check his breathing.'

'He's breathing. It's shallow but yes.'

Hannah knelt down and took Thomas' pulse. She nodded and then without saying anything quickly checked his pupils. 'No problems there. The most likely explanation is that he simply fainted but we need to put him in the coma position.' She rolled him onto his side and placed his arm under his head.

'Now we wait,' said Daniel trying to sound as calm and professional as his wife. 'He looked terrified when he saw me. How could a bird be in the attic, and more to the point why would it attack him?'

'I don't know Daniel. At the moment we need to just make sure he's okay.' She'd just finished speaking when Thomas opened his eyes.

'What happened? How come you're both standing there?'

'You fainted,' she said laconically. He tried to get up but she held him down. 'You need to take it slowly. Now, take your time and don't do anything until we say so.'

'I'm alright.'

'No Thomas. You need to listen to me. Before you stand I want you to sit up slowly. I'll grab a chair and then after a few moments put your head on your knees. It'll help the blood flow back to your head.' Thomas followed his mother's instructions and soon he began to feel somewhat better. He was still woozy but the spinning had stopped.

'You need to lie down and take things quietly for a while. Let me know when you're ready okay?'

A few minutes later Thomas was sitting up in bed and having a Drink of water. He felt foolish for having fainted but he couldn't get the image of the bird from his mind. He pulled himself up from the bed and slowly went down the stairs. As he did he heard his parents talking. Their voices were low and he wondered why they were almost whispering. He crept down a few more steps and, staining forward, tried to make out what they were saying.

He felt as if he was spying on them but something in the tone of their voices had sounded odd. He crept down to the bottom step and sat down. Still he couldn't hear them. He risked edging a few metres into the hallway and trying not to feel guilty, he leant forward.

'I know what you mean, Hannah,' he heard his father say, but I think it's just a bit fantastic that some sort of bird would attack him like that. Is it possible that he panicked and banged his head and thought he saw something and came to the wrong conclusion?'

'I suppose it's possible but he's not the type to be given to flights of fancy. But I agree it does seem strange. And you said that you were certain that there was no way a bird could get into the attic?' she asked.

Thomas knew that the longer he stayed on the stairs the greater the risk of being found. Feeling both dizzy and foolish he hid in the small store room on the stair landing and leaving the door a little ajar continued to listen.

'It's been a while since I was there but after he went to bed I shone the torch around. It was only a quick look but I couldn't see a bird anywhere.' He waited as Hannah sat in her chair looking at him and he felt for a moment as if he were one of her patients.

'It may be good if both of you have a look in the attic tomorrow. He seemed really sacred. It will keep playing on his mind if he doesn't find out what happened. What are your thoughts?'

'If you think that's for the best then we will. Meanwhile I'll go up and see how he is. I'll go and grab a movie and we can all watch it together. It'll be good for all of us to watch something silly. He looked back at her and he saw how worried she really was. She had assumed her professional persona when dealing with Thomas but now, unusually, she seemed alone and suddenly fragile.

He returned to the room and stopped in front of her. 'Are you okay?' he asked. She smiled and held out her hand and he took it and kissed her on the back of her wrist. 'Do you remember the first time I did that? You . . .'

'I'll never forget it. You thought you were so romantic and I mucked it up because I couldn't stop laughing. I'm surprised that you even saw me again.' He smiled and kissed her on her cheek. He went to the stairs and saw the back of Thomas as he hurried up the stairway.

Thomas knew that he had been too slow. He stopped, and feeling like a fool waited for his father to speak. 'What have we here? A lost boy? A runaway who couldn't get past the last step?'

'I . . . I . . .

'Yes, go on. You're about to say you heard nothing.'

No. What I wanted to do was laugh.'

'Laugh?'

'At your clumsy romantic technique.'

'So you're the expert now on romance are you?'

'No but you have to admit it was funny.'

'After your mum laughed I felt like a real prat. Thank goodness I didn't give up otherwise you wouldn't be here.'

'Thanks Dad. Now I'll tell you what video we can watch.'

***

The next morning Thomas and his father had warily climbed the stairs once more to the attic. 'Take your time Thomas. We don't want any mishaps today.' His father took out the old bulb and inserted the new one in the socket. Whilst it worked it was little better than the torches had been.

'I'll grab a stronger one. We'll finish up falling over. Come down and wait for me.'

'I'll be fine. Just don't take too long.'

'I don't think that's very wise. I think it's best to come down. There could be another bird.'

'You'll be back in a few minutes. I'm okay. Really.' He saw his father hesitate but he nodded and was gone. Thomas switched on the torch trying to find the dead bird. He thought he had killed it near the entrance. He shone his torch in the direction of where he thought he'd killed the bird, and to his surprise he saw it straight away.

It was the biggest crow that he had ever seen. Even in death it seemed to hold a remnant of its menace. He heard his father come back and he quickly installed the new globe and switched it on. 'Can you pick it up please dad? I know I should but . . .'

'Fair enough. You found it. I'll pick it up. Sounds like a fair deal to me.' He shuffled towards the bird and bent to pick it up. As he reached for it opened its eyes and stared at him with malevolence. Astonished he dropped it and it flew towards Thomas. Thomas yelled as it flew at his face.

He ducked but was too slow. The bird pecked his face and he cried out in pain. Thomas's father stumbled towards Thomas cursing as he was restricted by the height of the attic's roof. The bird turned towards him and then with a screech it flew at him.

Unprepared he was too late to protect himself. The bird viciously tore at his flesh and he screamed as it continued its frenetic attack. His face was pouring with blood. He collapsed and the bird sat on top of his head picking at his skull as if determined to destroy him.

Thomas cried out and to his relief found the courage to half run to his father. The bird saw him and ignoring him it continued viciously pecking at Daniel's head. The blood was now spurting from his head and Zerach heard his father moan and then his father was silent.

'Dad! Dad!' Thomas screamed as he attacked the bird with his fists. The bird looked at Thomas and looked back at his father. Zerach saw his opportunity and grabbed the bird. He was amazed at its strength as it fluttered in his hands but he grabbed its throat, and filled with triumph he slowly and deliberately strangled it.

He knelt down next to his dad and pulled him into a semi upright position. His father's body seemed too limp. He shook him and looked at his face and head. Somehow the bird's beak had done more damage than seemed possible. Thomas felt for his father's pulse. Feeling none, he started CPR and in spite of the tears that flowed down his face he forced himself to remember what he had been taught. Counting out loud he commenced the procedure. Two breaths, thirty compressions. He continued to count out and wanted to scream out for his mother's help but he had an irrational fear that any interruption would somehow prove fatal.

Time passed and he was feeling exhausted. Increasingly desperate, he blew harder then forced himself to stop. Perhaps, he reasoned, he needed to make the compressions harder. He increased his pressure and felt his father's rib break.

By now he was saturated with sweat and knew that he was unable to continue any longer. His arms were leaden and he was dizzy with having to do the breaths correctly. He stood not knowing what to do. If he left his father he could die. If he didn't leave him he knew that he didn't have enough strength to continue. He had to decide. Any time wasted could, he knew be fatal.

'Decide. Decide!' He clambered down the ladder and ran into the lounge room. 'Mum! Mum! Quick. Dad needs your help.' Hearing no answer, he ran through the house desperately trying to find her. Then he realised. Every Tuesday she had made it a point to dead head the roses in their huge, rambling garden.

He ran out the back door and saw her bright, blue Dress about fifty metres from the house. Cupping his hands around his mouth he yelled again. This time she looked up and he bellowed: 'Mum. It's dad. He's been attacked. He's in the attic.' She rushed up the gravel path and stood panting in front of him. 'What?'

'We have to get to the attic. Dad's been attacked. I tried CPR but he's not . . .' Without waiting for his answer, she ran to the house she clambered up the stairs with Thomas following a few steps behind her.

'Thomas, where is he?'

'But he was right there. Exactly where the bird is. I killed it. He was there Mum.'

'Then he's obviously got up and gone back down the stairs. He can't have been as bad as you thought.'

'Mum he was there. There's no way he could just come down the stairs. He had blood pouring down his face and he had no pulse. How can he get up?'

'I don't know. Perhaps he's tried to crawl out and got confused. Shine your torch. Look everywhere. He walked carefully around the arctic shining his torch into tiny spaces that he knew no one could possibly fit. Everywhere he looked all he could see were spider webs and mouse Droppings. In spite of his thoroughness it was obvious that his father had gone.

'I can't see him. I looked everywhere. He must have . . . but I don't see how he could . . .'

'We don't have time to waste. If he's not here then he must have got down the attic stairs. If he was as bad as you say I don't know how, but there's no other explanation. Come. We need to find him now.

He may be suffering from shock and got disorientated and wandered off somewhere. If he's bleeding as bad as you said then there may be traces of blood we can follow.' Without waiting for him to answer she went down the steps and stood for a moment on the landing. She looked down at the tiles but could see no traces of any blood.

'How badly was he bleeding?'

'Really badly. The bird kept on pecking and pecking at him. It was horrible. I stood there for a while and did nothing to help him.'

'We don't have time for guilt Thomas. We have to find him. Shock can kill people. It he's as bad as you say then he can't have got too far although I can't understand why there's no blood.'

'Could he have stopped it somehow? Perhaps he found something up in the attic and used it to staunch the blood.'

'It's possible but deep cuts take quite a while to stop. Come on. You look downstairs and I'll look upstairs. Wait. Of course. Where would you go if you were bleeding?'

'The bathroom.' They rushed to the bathroom but it was empty.

'He may have gone to the one downstairs,' said Thomas. They rushed downstairs but that too was empty.

'This is ridiculous. How can someone who's bleeding so badly not leave one drop of blood. I don't understand. We need to stop for a moment and think. Where else would he go?'

'He might try to find you. You're the doctor,' he said suddenly excited and full of hope. 'He knows that you were cutting back the roses. If he was in trouble he'd look for you.'

'Clever boy. I bet that's what he's done. Come on.'

They went out into the garden and started calling for him. They could hear their voices echoing back to them from the granite hill that sat behind the house like a rampart. As they called they searched the garden but found nothing.

Five minutes passed, then ten. Their yells were becoming more and more frantic and after twenty minutes their vocal cords could barely function. 'He can't just disappear into thin air. He may have fallen into the scrub and lost consciousness. Come on. We'll go back to the door and search under every bush, every tree every patch of ground until we find him.'

Thomas heard the panic that had started to edge into her voice. She had managed to maintain her professional persona but he knew that she wouldn't be able to stave off her emotions indefinitely.

They continued calling out his name but each cry sounding feebler than the last. Thomas grabbed a stick and she following his example began prodding into the thickets and rampant growth that had, over the years, gotten more and more out of control. They pushed their way through the dense scrub and forced their way through a thicket of wild blackberries that covered them both in deep scratches but still couldn't find him.

The sun had begun to sink closer to the horizon and the light began to fade. Finally, the sun blazed orange and then began it set. No sooner had in gone down then the mosquitoes started whining around their faces and biting their arms and hands. Soon it was too dark to see and suddenly Hannah stopped and started to weep.

'Oh Daniel, Daniel, where are you?' It was hard for Thomas to bear the grief he felt and the despair that he saw was beginning to creep into his mother. He went to her and placed his head on her shoulder as she continued to sob. He felt her take a long, slow breaths and he knew how hard it was for her to control herself.

'We need help. You keep looking and I'll ring triple zero. We can't do this alone.' She punched in the numbers and a woman answered the phone. 'Which service do you require?'

'Police.' She was put through and quickly gave the details of their adDress and a summary of what had happened. 'We need to go back to the house and wait until they arrive. It's too dark out here and they'll need us to fill them in on what happened. I presume they'll organise a search but I'm not sure how quickly they respond to these situations.'

Thomas took her hand and together they walked back to the house. As they did the mosquitoes fed on them relishing the unexpected banquet that had fallen their way.

CHAPTER SIXTEEN

The police had been kind and considerate but nevertheless the questions had gone on for hours. They had mainly focussed on Thomas. It was he who had witnessed the bird attacking his father. No matter how many times Thomas repeated what had happened they would nod sagely and then press on with more questions.

'I know how hard this must be for you both but I can't seem to get my head around how you say a dead bird suddenly came to life and attacked your dad. Obviously, it had to have been alive to attack him but you said that you killed it the day before. Are you sure Thomas it was dead?'

'I'm sure it was dead but dead birds don't suddenly come back to life. It doesn't make any sense,' Thomas said. She looked at her notebook and re-read some of what she had written earlier. 'You said that you gave your father CPR thinking that he had been severely injured by the bird. Then, when you couldn't revive him, you and your mother went up to the attic and he'd disappeared. As you know, we've searched every inch of the attic but there's nothing there. No dad, no bird, nothing at all.'

She looked at Hannah and reluctantly asked: 'you thought that it was about four hours or so that you looked for your husband. Is that right Dr Weinstock?'

'I can't say exactly, but it was for a long time. At first, as I said earlier, we thought that he must have gone to the bathroom but when he wasn't there we assumed that he went outside looking for me. I've told you this already. I don't understand why you're going over everything again.'

'Because, Dr Weinstock, people forget details. And it's often in the details where we find clues. But to be honest there seems to be no clues here at all. As you said there were no traces of blood anywhere even though your son said he was bleeding quite badly. He seemed to be in a very bad state. Yet somehow he got up and walked to the garden and we can't find him. The dogs have found nothing and neither have the police who've been searching. We'll come back tomorrow when we can see better in the daylight. At the moment, I'm sorry to say there's not much more we can do for now.'

She looked at her sergeant who had said little but Hannah knew that she was a woman who missed nothing. Every word, every gesture was being watched, assessed and analysed to be filed away and mulled over until she found what piece of the puzzle was missing.

The policewomen stood up and Hannah and Thomas went with them to the front door. 'We'll be here at first light in the morning. The dog squad will be back as will a senior detective. I know it's a silly thing to say but try to get some rest. I know that you won't get much sleep but sitting up all night going over every detail isn't going to help. I'm sorry if I'm talking in platitudes but I don't know what else to say.'

She looked at her sergeant as she put away her note book and the sergeant took Hannah gently by her elbow. 'This has been a terrible shock. Frankly I'm surprised that the dogs couldn't pick up his scent. Once it's light we'll stand a much better chance. I'll see you in the morning.'

Thomas closed the door unsure as what to do. His mother saw his confusion and gave him a hug. 'Come into the kitchen and I'll make you a cup of tea or coffee. It'll give me something to do. I can't eat anything but do you want me to get you something?'

'Coffee thanks mum but I feel guilty sitting here Drinking coffee when dad's out there lost. He heard the whistle of the kettle and the water being poured into the mugs.

'Oh shit, shit, shit,' cried Hannah as the cups crashed down onto the floor. She bent down to clear up the mess. 'I'm sorry Thomas. I feel so lost and helpless. I don't know how I'm going to get through until tomorrow morning. If there was only something more we could do but . . . but . . .'

Suddenly she grabbed the torch off the top of the fridge and turning to Thomas she said: 'There's absolutely no way I'm going to stand in the kitchen Drinking coffee while Daniel is out there lost. If there's one chance in a thousand, then I'm prepared to try.'

'I'm coming with you,' he said.

'Okay. Grab the other torch and let's go. Get the mosquito repellent and give yourself a good spray and then I'll do the same. It'll be one less thing to worry about.'

They walked out to the garden and the moon gave out a feeble glow but it was better than **nothing** and their torches made twin peaks of light as they once again started their search.

'I think we need to go further down the garden where the creek starts. I know we couldn't have possibly looked under every tree or shrub but we need to widen our search. He must have gone further though why, God only knows.'

They picked up the two sticks that they had used before and started checking under the foliage of every tree and bush they could see. They heard the startled screech of the little Corella's as they flew in their hundreds from the shelter of the trees and they could make out their white shapes as they circled above them in confusion.

A small mob of kangaroos fled into the night and as Thomas shone his torch at one it stood there mesmerised by the light until he moved the beam from it and it bounded off into the semi-bushland that now surrounded them.

They could hear the gurgle of the creek and the croaking of the frogs which abruptly stopped when they heard their footsteps. 'Do you think we should split up? Thomas asked, 'We'll be able to cover a larger area.'

'No Thomas. I'm not risking losing you as well. We'll stay together no matter what.' They continued to look and as they left the area of the creek the frogs started their rasping song. The Corella's after a few squabbles had returned and roosted in the blue gums that dotted the property.

As they continued to walk they came to a rough path. One branch led to the left the other bent slightly to the right. 'Which way mum?'

'I wish I knew. You're guess is as good as mine.'

'Left,' he said and as soon as he said it he felt he should have said right but decided to stay silent. Vacillating was not going to achieve anything and as they had no clues one direction was as good as another.

They continued looking but the torch batteries were beginning to run out. Trying to ignore the loss of light they pressed on and came to a large River Red Gum whose gnarled trunk made it appear both foreign and sinister. They shone their torches into its hollowed out interior. Thomas crouched down and they heard the furious hissing of a feral cat. Its teeth, sharp and blood stained glimmered in their torch lights. It hissed its contempt and dashed off into the bush.

They continued onward occasionally calling out Daniel's name but again their calls were lost in the darkness. Time passed and they knew that soon their batteries would run out of power.

'We can't risk the batteries dying. We'd find it very hard to make our way back. We tried Thomas. We really tried. Even though we couldn't find him I'm pleased to say that we didn't sit in the kitchen miserable and ineffective but we did our best.'

Just then her torch went out and they turned to head back. With one poorly working torch it was becoming harder to retrace their steps and the bush that seemed quite benign during the day now seemed menacing.

'Is this the right way?' Hannah asked as she and Thomas became more confused.

'I think so. If we can find that big, old tree we'll know and then be able to get our bearings.' They set off again and a possum dashed across the path and then disappeared down a gap in the side of a small hill that they had not noticed before.

'How did we miss this? asked Thomas.

'We didn't. We would have to have seen it before. It's small but distinctive. I wonder if your dad got this far?' She looked at Thomas and he saw the beginnings of real fear on her face. She was, he knew, facing the dreadful possibility that the bush, that **had surrounded** them for so long ignored by them, could swallow them up as it appeared to have done to Daniel.

'It feels like we're intruders but I think we need to look around the hill,' Thomas said.

'We know that the battery is not going to last much longer but I'm prepared to chance it.'

She took her hand in his and they edged their way over the rocky hill occasionally stumbling as the rocks shifted under their feet and the smaller stones threatened their balance as they slowly ascended. Suddenly a rock under Thomas's foot came adrift and he fell to the ground. His torch tumbled away from him and he lunged at it and managed to stop it rolling. Thomas crawled to it and it was then that he saw something yellow. It was his father's favourite colour and the colour of the shirt he'd been wearing that morning.

'Mum! Mum!' he yelled. 'It's a piece of dad's shirt. I'm sure of it' He looked towards his mother and she fell to her knees and held the fragment in her hand. She held it for a moment and smelled it. She knew it was Daniel's.

'Shine the torch. It's his. I bought him **this** shirt at the street market last year. He can't be far away.' She hugged him and they felt the thrill of having found evidence that he was nearby. As they held the fragment he noticed that **another piece of the shirt** was just outside what appeared to be a cave that had been dug into the hill. Excited and elevated he started to crawl into it when his mother yelled. 'Thomas stop! I think that we've reached where the old tin mines used to be. They've been abandoned for over a hundred years. They can go for miles and some of them are so deep that . . . that . . .'

She didn't need to say any more. Thomas knew what she thought. His dad had crawled in to find shelter and in his confusion had fallen down a mine shaft. And that could only mean one of two things. His father had fallen down a deep shaft and had been killed or, at best, was lost in the maze of tunnels that burrowed thorough the old mine field.

'I'm not going back to the house Thomas. I know it ridiculous but if I go I feel like I've given up on him. It's totally irrational but I won't change my mind. I want you to go home and show the piece of shirt to the police. They'll need it for the dogs. His scent will still be on it'

'I won't go. I'm staying with you. I'm not leaving dad here. What if he calls out and you can't hear him? What then?'

'Thomas there's no perfect solution. It's essential that the police know where the mines are. They can send their experts down and look. I know how hard it is but you must go back. Take my scarf. It's getting cold and you'll need it.'

"But what about you?'

'I'll be fine. **Just go**. Don't waste time disagreeing with me.'

He knew that what she had said was the most sensible thing to do but, as he waved a feeble goodbye to his mother he felt that he was betraying his father and the further away he walked from the mine the worse he felt.

He put the piece of shirt in his pants pocket hoping that his own scent would not confuse the dogs. He desperately wanted to hold the material himself. It would bring some tiny hint of comfort but he resisted and continued in the direction he thought that their house might be.

No sooner had he turned away, when the moon, as if on cue disappeared behind a cloud and the night turned a deeper shade of grey. He wondered if he too would lose himself in the **tangled mass of trees**.

The torch's globe gave a little shimmer and stopped working. Now his task seemed almost impossible. He forced himself to try to remember each small detail of the way that they'd come. Could he recognise anything that would help him?

He felt close to panic but he forced it down. He had read of the dangers of people who were lost when they panicked and the consequences of their actions were too often fatal. He would not, could not fail.

He stumbled on and tripped on a small branch that lay on the path. The moon as if taking pity of him peeked out from the clouds and he saw that it had been broken in two.

It was still in one piece but clearly part of it had partly sheared off and he felt a flutter of hope. He used his stick to see if he could find other branches or twigs that had been broken or damaged. After about ten minutes of walking he felt a branch beneath him and put it to his face, it too was damaged. He knew that he was going the right way.

Finally, he came to the fork in the path and he grew more confident. Soon he heard the gurgling of the creek and the ever-present sound of the frogs. He knew where he was. He would, he now knew, be able to get home.

CHAPTER SEVENTEEN

He saw the roof of his house its chimney shimmering above the roof like ancient beacon in the moonlight. Soon he was at the house and he went into the dark kitchen. After fumbling for a moment found the light switch and turned it on.

He felt hungry and felt as if his body was betraying him. He should be unable to eat. He should be grief stricken but his body needed food and its needs were more urgent then his feelings. He tried to ignore his hunger but he could almost hear his father's voice saying: 'Listen to your body mate. We all live too much in our bloody heads especially a maths geek like me.'

He ached with longing. He longed to hear his father's voice not just in his head but each syllable as he spoke it. Each inflection of his father's deep voice and its special cadence, as if each word he spoke was the result of some complicated algebraic problem.

He went to the fridge and looked inside. Milk, left over mashed potato, a few tomatoes and some cold pizza. He grabbed the pizza and heated it in the microwave oven and waited for it to give out its peculiar little "ding" that they'd all laughed at the first time they had heard it.

He bit into it and chewed, but it tasted of despair. He spat it out and grabbed the carton of milk and took a swig and that too tasted like nothing but he made himself Drink it. He felt himself beginning to shake and he took the throw off the battered lounge chair. He put the throw over his shoulders and wanted to light he wood fire but was too tired. He knew that he should take a shower but the effort seemed too much. He sat and thought of his mother outside on the dark mourning or at least desperate to find her husband.

He knew that it was pointless to sit and become obsessed with his mother. Should he try to at least lie down? He knew he wouldn't sleep but the thought of drawing his duvet over his head and cocooning himself in his bed was a comforting thought and he made his way upstairs to his room.

He climbed into his bed, not caring that his clothes were filthy and then he remembered that he still had the piece of shirt in his pocket. He knew he should leave it but he needed to touch it. **He longed** to bring his father, just that tiny bit closer to him if only for a few seconds.

He took it out and held it to his face and then smelt it. His father's special smell lingered and it was then that he knew he could no longer hold back the tears and he wept as if he were a child which indeed he was. The child of two parents who had always loved him unconditionally and he had assumed always would.

The moon shone through his window and he wished it would magically turn into a full moon so that his mother would have some comfort. The night passed but he didn't sleep. He checked his mobile and read the time, **4:30** it said with its usual certainty, a certainty he felt he'd now lost forever.

The night dragged to its end and the morning sun shone through his window. He was glad that its rays would be of some comfort to his mother as she kept her vigil outside of the mines.

He was about to get up when he heard a knock at the door and he knew at once who it would be. They had said that they would arrive early and they had. He rushed down and opened the door and let them in.

'We've found piece of his shirt,' he blurted out before they could say anything. He took it out and the new sergeant put on a pair of rubber gloves. She handed it to the policeman who was in charge of the two German Shepherds which he held with expert ease.

'Where?' she asked. He was surprised at her abruptness but then realised that this was a woman for whom **words** were superfluous and that if anyone could find his father **then** she would.

'Tell me as we walk. I want to know everything's that happened. I don't care how important it seems or does not. I need it all.'

He walked downs the gravel path with her at his side and the dogs had already started sniffing after the handler had placed it briefly under their black noses. He told her everything that he could remember and it was only when he mentioned the word tin mine that she looked truly worried.

He knew that the mines had added an unexpected complication to what was already an unusual disappearance. He knew at once what she thought. She concealed her expression with a near perfect mask, but his heightened senses knew that she was more concerned than she had been when she had climbed out of the car just ten minutes earlier.

'Can you remember the way?' she asked. He nodded. If he could find his way back in the dark getting there now would be reasonably straightforward. The woman, who still hadn't give him her name kept silent but he saw that she was taking note of everything like a moving camera capturing pictures that she could replay at will.

He looked to see what the dogs were doing. He had expected that they'd pick up the scent quickly after all, it hadn't rained and they had the scent from the shirt. If his father had gone this way why hadn't they found his odour.

Should he ask or keep quiet? **However, he decided say nothing and** to focus on arriving at the mine entrance as quickly as possible. After about a half an hour he found the giant gum and pointed it out to her.

'We're not too far away. I remember this tree and not too far from her is a small hill which we missed the first time and then we ….'

'Tell me later Thomas, let's **just** get there eh?'

He felt foolish but knew that she was right. The excited ramblings of a teenage boy were not what she wanted to hear. She wanted to see the mine and words were holding her up.

'There!' he said. 'There's the hill and mum will be waiting outside for us.' He ran ahead and arrived at the mine entrance. His mother had gone.

CHAPTER EIGHTEEN

'She was there! Just outside the entrance. There's a little hole but it was hard to see in the dark and our torches were running out but I know this is the right spot.'

'Could you have got confused in the dark? After all there wasn't much moonlight last night and there must be more than one mine entrance. I imagine that they all look similar.'

'It's the right one. I know it is. Mum was just here.' He stood where he had seen her last and waited. She must believe him, he thought but then he realised that even if he was right then where was his mother?

'Mum! Mum!' he yelled.' He heard his voice disappear into the bush and the **little** corellas took off and careered across the perfect blue sky their joy and freedom a cruel reminder of everything he felt he had lost.

'Mum!' He turned to the woman and he saw the sympathy in her eyes but also, he knew she was calculating how easy it would be for a distressed boy to be confused.

'Listen to me Thomas. This is very important. I need to be blunt. As you know, if your father is in the mine and he went in during the night time I'd say that the chances of him falling down a shaft are fairly high. I can't be certain but it is the most likely explanation. If, and I don't think this is the case, if he's in there then there is still hope. **The dogs, as you know haven't picked up any other scents. Do you have anything on you that belongs to your mother?'**

'The scarf! She gave it to me when she said she wasn't going to leave him. I didn't want to take it but she said I needed it.'

'Do you have it with you?'

'Yes. It's in my pants pocket. I took it off when I got home and put it in the opposite pocket to dad's shirt. I wanted to have each of them in a different pocket. One each side of me.'

She reached out and touched his cheek. 'That was a lovely thing to do. Now if you give it to me Paul our dog handler can give it to the dogs and they'll know if your mum was in the area.' He handed it over and Paul put it in front of the dog's noses. They strained at their leds and sniffed about excitedly then stopped and wagged their tails.

'Got her,' Paul said.

'You're sure?'

'Yes absolutely,' Paul said. 'She was here. There can be no doubt about that. She may have wandered off but given the reason she stayed here that seems unlikely.'

'I agree,' said the woman.

'Then where is she?' asked Thomas.

'Your mother is in the mine,' she said. 'She's decided to try to find him herself.'

'But she said that she'd wait for me and now she's gone. I don't think I . . . I . . .'

He would not allow himself to cry or become angry but he felt as if his mother had deserted him and gone back on her word. He was, however, after a brief internal struggle able to realise that he would have done the same thing himself. Standing outside of the mine whilst someone you loved needed you, would override any other consideration. 'I don't even know your name.

'I'm sorry Thomas. I should have told you when we first met. My name is Sophia. Sophia Garcia. My grandparents came from Mexico.'

'May I call you Sophia?'

'Of course, you can. It means wisdom but it's a name that takes a bit of living up to. Lucky for me not too many people know what it means.'

'But you're wise. I can tell and your wisdom will find mum and dad.' He knew that he sounded overly naïve and trusting but he didn't care. She looked at him and he saw her compassion. He knew that she was special. How he knew he couldn't understand but he felt that it was not pure chance that led her to him and his family.

'I think it's time to see if your mum's in there don't you?'

'Yes,' he said. He wanted to say more but couldn't think of what to say and the sooner they started the better. Paul took the dogs closer to the mine. He heard them whine and he knew that Sophia had been correct.

'We've got a problem,' Paul said to Sophia as the dogs continued to whine. 'I don't know how anyone could get in there. There's hardly any space.'

Paul Dropped to his knees and forced his way into the hole and to their surprise he disappeared. Thomas wished that it was him looking for his mother and not some stranger but he knew that was impossible.

They heard a cry and Paul emerged. He **was filthy but his expression** said it all. Thomas felt sick. What could that look mean? Sophia lent closer to Paul but Thomas couldn't hear what was being said.

'What did you find? Are mum and dad okay?' Paul was about to answer when Sophia stopped him by putting her hand on his shoulder. 'He can't see much but he saw enough to discover that there are multiple tunnels, perhaps ten or more. They could be anywhere in there. That means this is going to take longer than we thought. They may be together although the probability of that seems unlikely'

Thomas nodded not sure what to say or do. How would the police proceed from here he wondered? How many people would it take to find his parents in what seemed like a rabbit warren?

'I know how hard this is for you Thomas. But, at the risk of sounding clichéd, we still have a lot of resources that we can use. We have police who are trained for most eventualities and I'm sure that we can find extra personnel who'll help. It may take a while but it will happen as soon as we can organise it.'

'And if you can't find them. What then?'

'It's too soon to be thinking like that. Your mum was here a few hours ago and for all we know . . .'

She was interrupted by the sudden whining of the dogs. Paul looked at Sophia and she walked over and spoke to Paul who was grinning madly. Thomas rushed over and Sophia smiled and patted him on his back. 'The dogs have heard something. We need to be really quiet and to listen.'

They huddled around the entrance and desperately tried to hear what the dogs had heard. Paul stopped the whining of the dogs and the three of them squashed together all of them straining to hear something.

A minute passed. The another. Thomas flinched. He'd thought he could detect something but it was so faint that he couldn't be sure. 'I've heard something but I can't be sure. Perhaps I'm imagining it because I want to hear something and . . .'

'Thomas you need to be quiet,' he heard Sophia say. 'Don't try to second guess yourself. We need one person to go in. Thomas, you're the smallest so it makes sense for you to go. Paul is going to hold you by your ankles that way you won't be tempted to go too far in yourself.'

'But I can go further in than the length of my body! I'll be able to . . .'

'Potentially get yourself lost. Two people lost are bad. Three's a disaster. And don't be tempted to wriggle free.' Reluctantly he agreed and he pushed through the hole into the gloom.

He knew that Paul said that there was some light but he could hardly see a thing. He stretched out his body and felt Paul's hands holding him and to his shame he felt relieved that he didn't have to go in too far.

He had now gone in as far as he could and the darkness seemed to be increasing at a rate that didn't make sense. It had been gloomy, and then gradually it grew darker. Now it was almost black and he felt a shiver run down his spine. Something strange was happening as he could feel a sudden blast of cold air.

He started to shiver as the temperature plummeted. He felt his mind grow numb. He felt his hope dissipated like a deflated balloon and then the doubt and fear increased. He felt the first oozing of despair. He was in a place that held no hope, no life and a blackness that was unimaginable.

He wanted to scream but even the act of breathing now seemed a waste of time. He felt a dark power pulling him ever downwards. 'Shouldn't we have heard something buy now? Paul asked Sophia.

'Give him a few more seconds then drag him out.'

Thomas felt the blackness pulling at him and he was consumed with despair. He tried to fight it but how could he fight something like this. Something that had no name and something that reached into his soul sucking out his will to live.

Vainly he tried again but he knew that he was losing a battle that he couldn't comprehend. He grew weaker and he felt his will to live flicker out. He remembered his parents and their love and he wept believing that he would never see them again. He would never again see the sun or the blue of an Australian sun.

It was then that he saw a tiny light. It was weak but it was there. He thought that he was hallucinating but gradually the light grew and he saw it take shape. It looked **like coloured circles** that now hovered over him and bathed him in their light. He felt the darkness recoil as it tried to fight off the spheres. He felt its hatred and sensed its torment then it was gone.

Outside Sophia smiled and as she did he heard his mother's voice.

CHAPTER NINETEEN

Hannah's ribs were sore but the medics had determined that apart from some bruising and slight dehydration she was well enough to recuperate at home. Thomas had surprised himself by being able to push his father's disappearance to the back of his mind as he fussed over his mother who had said hardly a word to him as to what had happened to her.

He wondered if she too had felt what he had felt when he was trying to find her but said nothing. He knew that she would say that he had suffered from a hallucination caused by his acute distress. He knew however, that it had been real and if it wasn't for the lights appearing he would have been consumed.

The next day his mother had slowly climbed out of bed and went into the kitchen. She didn't feel hungry but she made a piece of toast and forced herself to eat it. She added another shot to her coffee and she heard the printer in the study printing out sheets of paper.

'What are you printing?'

'I know it probably won't make any difference but when I couldn't sleep last night I thought that we can't be a hundred percent certain that dad is in the mine. He saw that she was about to interject but he quickly continued; 'He could be somewhere else. He may have amnesia or something and if he is, there's no one looking for him, except in the mine.'

'But the piece of shirt by the entrance. You can't ignore that.'

'I know but he may have stayed there for a while and then left. I'm going to put these posters up on every post and bus stop that I can. If I'm wrong then it doesn't matter but I'll be doing something and that's better than sitting around doing nothing. I have to try Mum.'

He grabbed his backpack and carefully placed the posters in the bag. He went outside and was soon peddling down the road stopping every fifty metres and taping the posters on sign posts and electricity poles.

He peddled on and was by now a long way from his home. He found himself in a suburb whose tree lined streets gave him the opportunity to place the last few precious posters on their mottled trunks.

He was exhausted but was pleased with his efforts. He had already posted dozens of messages on his Face book page but no-one had seen his father. He looked at the last poster and touched his father's face tenderly and felt tears welling in his eyes. He turned around and headed towards his home.

As he did a young man sat in the front seat of his dad's car. He noticed the posters that were festooned along the road. Intrigued, he pushed his face closer to the window. Curious he tapped his father on the arm. He'd been thinking about Rueben and what he'd said to him. It seemed strange for he'd pushed Reuben into the back of his mind. It had been too confusing to understand but he suddenly remembered what Reuben had said about finding the other three. As he was lost in his reverie he noticed a series of posters that were festooned along the street. Normally he would have ignored them but as he looked he felt that he was somehow being pulled towards them.

'There's dozens of those posters. Someone is really keen to get something or someone back. I know it sounds a bit dumb but can you stop? I just want to have a quick look.'

'Why would you want to look at some random poster? I don't get it.'

'Just humour me please dad.' His father pulled the car over and stopped. The young man got out and walked over to the tree. He saw what didn't seem possible. He went closer and looked at the photo of the young man underneath the photo of his father. He read what it said but his vision had grown hazy for he was looking at a photo that looked exactly like him. It was as if he were looking in a mirror and seeing himself.

He felt giddy as he remembered that **Reuben had said that he would find his twin**. It had started and he felt both a thrill of discovery and a sense of Dread. His spheres had somehow led him here and he was intelligent enough to know that the meaning of Thomas was "twin."

CHAPTER TWENTY

Thomas sat at the breakfast table playing with a poached egg his mother had made for him. He pushed his fork into it and as the orange yoke oozed out and knew that eating was impossible. He waited for his mother to encourage him but she too had not eaten. He wished he had the words to comfort her but knew that it wasn't possible. She took a tiny sip of her coffee, and her mind, he knew was in the mine with her husband.

Two days had passed and in spite of all of the searching nothing had been found. No clues, no hints, no more scents to guide the dogs. It was as if Daniel had been swallowed by the earth.

As each day passed he knew how hard it was for his mother to force herself from her bed. Once she had achieved this her routine was always the same. She would slowly walk back to the mine where she would sit and fret over everything that was happening.

He too, had spent time at the mine but after two visits he knew that he couldn't return. He kept on having flashbacks to his terror and the thought that his father, if he were conscious and in fact in the mine that he too may have been crushed by the dark force that had so nearly claimed him.

It was an unbearable thought and to compensate he spent his time running of hundreds of posters as if he were possessed. The third day arrived. Still nothing. They'd stopped trying to eat at the table. The charade of normality couldn't be sustained. Thomas would sit on the battered lounge chair eating an occasional Dry cracker and his mother seemed to exist on coffee alone.

It was eleven in the morning when Hannah's mobile rang. She had added Sophia's name to her address book so she knew it was her who was ringing. She let it ring. If she ignored it then she wouldn't have to hear if that her husband was still missing or worse dead. A part of her still believed that he was alive. But as each day passed her fear increased and she struggled to **feign** a vague pretence of optimism for Thomas's sake.

It rang again and again and at last Thomas couldn't bear it. 'Mum! You have to answer it. You know you do.' She looked at him and the resemblance between her son and her husband was so similar that she had to look away. The phone continued to ring and at last she answered it.

'It's Sophia, Hannah. There's nothing more I would like to say than that we found him but unfortunately, we haven't. We searched as much as we can and have had experts climbing down shafts but apart from bit and pieces left over from the miners there's nothing. We're beginning to think that he may have gone somewhere else after he went in. I think it's time we called the press and the TV stations and report that fact that he's missing. If he left the mine then someone may have seen him. Is that okay with you?'

'Please do wherever you think will help but I'm not up to giving an interview. I'm struggling as it is.'

'It's your choice Hannah. The main thing is to get his face out into the public arena and to use the mass media without disrupting your life too much. The reporters will phone you so I suggest you let all your calls go to your message bank and ignore them. I'll get onto this straight away. 'It'll be on the news tonight.' 'His photo and details will be on TV tonight and in the paper in the morning. Don't answer the phone and don't open the door unless it's the police. There's only so much I can deal with so please do ask.'

Thomas had many questions he wanted to ask but he saw that his mother, like himself, was suffering and kept quiet. All that was left for them was to wait and neither of them knew how that was going to be possible.

CHAPTER TWENTY ONE

'Are you sure you want to watch the news Thomas? It's hard enough as it is. It could make us feel worse.'

'I have to. I don't want to but I have to.' She pulled his legs off the lounge and sat next to him and they switched the TV on. The first ten minutes of the news was taken up with the latest sporting controversy and the rest to other world news. The news reader paused and a photo of Daniel appeared behind the newsreader.

'Dr Weinstock the well known mathematician has been missing for nearly a **week and fears are mounting for his safety.** The police suspect that he may have fallen in an abandoned mine shaft that is situated at the rear of his property. Locals say that they have been asking for years for barriers to have been erected but their pleas have been ignored. In a strange coincidence, Dr Weinstock' great grandfather disappeared from the same property some eighty years ago. Is this a bizarre case of history repeating itself? If anyone has any information that may be of help to the police please contact them.'

'Turn it off. I've seen enough. What are they implying? His grandfather has nothing to do with it. The bloody media will go to any length to make ridiculous connections just to titillate the public. It makes me sick.'

She grabbed her phone and dialled Sophia. 'That's not what you said was going to happen. I thought it was a straight forward missing person story so that we could find anyone who may have seen him.

They've turned **it** into some second rate mystery with sinister links to the past. The bastards! How dare they treat him like this? I should never have agreed to this. Never.'

'Hannah. That's not what was supposed to have happened. I'm so sorry.'

'Goodbye Sophia.' Hannah glared at Thomas her eyes tight with anger.

'If you two hadn't acted like bloody boy scouts clambering around in the attic looking for a nonexistent bird none of this would have happened. I've managed to keep quiet up until now but not anymore. And **look** where your **boy's** own adventure has left us. It's left us with a missing husband and father. And to top it off we have this ludicrous sensationalistic nonsense about his great grandfather. Thank God that they didn't get hold of one of his ridiculous note books full of runes and symbols that meant nothing. It would have gone on for weeks and all the while where is Daniel? Can you answer me that Thomas? Can you?'

'Mum I'm sorry but how was I to know what was going to happen? I can't understand that somehow this is my fault. You're being really unfair.'

'I'm too angry to talk to you Thomas. The number of times I've heard your dad going on about those stupid runes and what they may have meant has driven me crazy. Did you know that your dad had this theory that it was some sort of message conveying the sacredness of numbers and he's supposed to be a maths professor? Its sheer lunacy.' She left the room and slammed the door behind her.

Thomas sat, speechless. All this time she had been blaming him and what did she mean about the runes? He put his head in his hands and after his anger had subsided he felt it. It was back. Despair was creeping up on him. After what his mother had just said he didn't know how to fight it and this time there were no circles of light to help him.

He knew that he needed to do something to **stop this creeping disease that** seemed to know exactly how to ooze, dark as oil, into his mind. It wasn't just his mind. His body was heavy and even the thought of getting out of the house seemed a task so challenging that it filled him with inertia. His stomach ached, not in pain but as if something heavy sat, fat boulders each one heavier than the last.

His mind now felt the first flush of anxiety, depression's brother who would wait until his mind exhausted then feed on him. **It was a parasite willing** to destroy itself and its host who happened to be called Thomas.

His mind was turning in on itself. Colours faded then dimmed to a dull grey. The light outside seemed feeble and even though the sky was blue to him it was as if it were covered in pitch. Round and round his thoughts went stuck in the rut of repetition, falling into the same pot holes, **potholes** that grew deeper each minute.

He heard the door open and his mother walked in. Her expression was full of guilt and she came to him and sat down next to him. She leant over and embraced him. He felt her love and he began to sob. Great gasping ugly sounds came from a part of him of which he was previously unaware. His sorrow seemed to have no limit.

His body rocked back and forward in a grief so profound he wondered how anyone could survive such pain. His posters now seemed pathetic scraps of paper pinned to posts and trees as if by a five year old looking for a lost pet. How pathetic he had been in his infantile optimism as he rode out each day his bag full of photos of his dad with his own tucked underneath his father's like an addendum.

She continued to hold him and then to his amazement she began to sing to him. It was his favourite song when he was three or four years old. He'd been convinced that the monsters under his bed were waiting to get him even though his night light was supposed to keep them at bay.

At first, he resisted. He was sixteen not an infant but her voice and the cadence and peace of the song soothed him and softened his pain. Gradually he stopped sobbing and he rubbed his sleeve against his face.

She continued singing and he felt a hint of hope as he remembered how the song had worked when he was little. He knew that it wasn't just the song; **it** was the love it contained. He leant over and kissed her cheek. She looked at him and her eyes too were full of tears.

'I'm sorry. I was so involved in my **own loss that** I didn't think about how hard this is for you as well. I know that you were in pain but had stupidly assumed because, unlike me, you were out every day putting up his photo. That you had hope and a sense of purpose. But that can only last so long can't it?'

He nodded and felt the darkness retreat but he knew it was a tactical withdrawal not a defeat. 'It's been a long time since I heard you sing that song. It always made me feel safe. Do you remember how terrified I'd get when you turned out the light in my room?'

'How could I forget? My God, what Daniel and I went through and goodness knows how many different lamps we tried but finally we found one that worked for you.'

'I can still remember it. It was the one with the stars on it and the patterned circles that used to go around and around like they were little planets. I loved it. It was like looking into infinity.'

'Come on. I'm going to make us a proper lunch and were both going to eat it. After that we'll have some ice cream and pie. Even though we feel sad we have to carry on. We can't simply give up. Now you can peel the vegetables and I'll make the stew. When we've finished you can wash up.' She smiled and he knew how hard it was for her to do what she had offered but they would eat and wait. It was all they could do.

Lunch finished they put the dishes away and Hannah rang Sophia. 'I'm sorry about before. It's been so hard that . . .'

'Hannah there's no need. I know how hard it is especially when all you can do is wait. It makes one feel so helpless.'

'Have you heard anything more after the TV and papers published his photo?'

'Not yet but we're still hopeful.'

Neither of them knew that it was the last positive thing that Sophia would be able to say to Hannah or Thomas. Days turned into weeks and then the first month went by and then another and still there was nothing.

Hannah and Thomas were now painfully beginning to be dimly aware that Daniel may never be found. It was an inconceivable prospect, but as the months continued their passage and the calendar silently announced that it was June, then July. Too slowly December had arrived and a year had passed.

Hannah had delayed any sort of memorial service but after the year had passed they had had a small ceremony. It had been shattering but they had got through it and it was then that Thomas's dreams began.

His depression lifted the day after the first Dream. The Dream was urgent and brutally simple. He had a twin. The twin was special and the twin recently discovered his name. He would **eventually find him.**

In his dream he saw his twin who was in an antique shop and a man whom **he somehow knew was called Reuben spoke to his twin.** 'I had hoped to see you in my shop again Zerach but the darkness is gathering strength more quickly than we had thought was possible. It's started to feed again and has fed briefly on your twin. You've seen his name in the posters. His father was taken by the darkness and tried to take your twin as well. Fortunately, his mother pulled him back but he has not fully healed. Only you and the four of you together can do that.

His name is as you learnt when you read the poster is Thomas Weinstock. Once you've found him you will find the others. Be brave. The battle is nearly on us. Take care, precious one.'

CHAPTER TWENTY TWO

Scarlett and Darcy

It was nine fifty on a humid Adelaide morning as Scarlet O'Neil sat at her desk looking out of the classroom window. The view was as boring as the lesson as she, along with twenty seven other year ten students, endured another session in the joys of algebra.

Her teacher was thin and had earned herself the name of 'The Praying Mantis,' a cruel but accurate description of the poor woman. Ms. Sayed's earnestness was never satisfied and consequently she had adopted the habit of tilting her head forward searching for any morsel of interest that a stray student might bestow. This image was reinforced by her clothes which were invariably dull and consisted of seven outfits that matched the days of the week.

'If you take the square of the . . .' she intoned as she scanned the room in a doomed attempt to attract a flicker of interest from her moribund class . . . you will find . . .'

Scarlet had however had heard nothing. She was too intent on her doodling which always seemed to take the same path. She would start with a circle and in it she would put smaller and smaller circles until it reached the centre which was represented by a dot. Once this was finished it was time to take out her coloured pencils to fill in the spaces. The outer was blue, followed by violet, then yellow, and finally white. When she had finished she smiled. It gave her a sense of relief from the trauma of her life which consisted of taking care of her disabled mother and her two younger brothers.

She had been their carer for over five years and in spite of her skills she'd lost control of Elliot and Fletcher whose hormones now ruled their lives and seemed to control their minds. Gone were the innocent, if occasionally difficult children to be replaced by two strangers who spent half of their lives looking at porn and who seemed to think, along with their peers, it was the normal thing to do.

She frowned and pushed the Drawing away from her and started another. This time she was determined to change the pattern. She had just started when she felt the atmosphere in the room change.

Scarlett looked behind her, and as she did, she felt the hairs on the back of her neck stand up. She started to turn around and had assumed that the other students would have also felt something sinister. It was as real and palpable as the desk in front of her. She could feel the darkness as it probed into her mind seeking out her vulnerability.

Ms. Sayed walked up to Scarlett and put her hand on Scarlett's shoulder. Scarlett was surprised at the strength of it and its surety. She felt the woman's power as it travelled along her body into a part of her she had always denied. She kept it hidden, this tiny spark of spirituality that she would never acknowledge. Yet she longed for with a yearning that would occasionally be rewarded with something beautiful. She would see the innocent incandescence of a rainbow lorikeet as it splashed in a pool of water sending out golden beams that made prisms of light in the air. It was something magical and moving. Then to see it take flight, it's flashing wings beating against the vivid blue of the perfect sky and land in the tree whose leaves still glistened with the shower that had fallen a few moments before.

She knew at these special times that such an appreciation of beauty was spiritual and lay in all humans if only they would allow it. Now, however, that small glow had deserted her. The shadow crept further into her. Even though she was in the classroom her mind had been forced backwards in time. She was at home trying to stop her bothers from fighting each other and had felt both angry and disillusioned with her futile attempts to stop them.

Scarlett was forced to revisit her own suffering. Each day she tried as always to be the peacemaker and the harder she tried it seemed the more she was derided. What she had kept suppressed for so long had been discovered. It reveals to her feelings of grief, loss and a pain that never seemed to leave her even when she smiled and joked with her exiled brethren. The two loners marooned in a concrete school with a thousand students.

She struggled against the feeling but knew it was taking hold. Getting stronger and blacker each minute. She felt the abyss that seemed to now wait as if it had waited for just this moment for this event to happen. She knew she was losing. She tried to think of happy events. A childhood party but instead of joy all she could recall was her brothers having a food fight with the birthday cake as she sat pretended to be amused whilst inside she saw her tiny part destroyed.

'Stay still child,' Ms. Sayed said. Her voice had changed and as Scarlett looked up she felt a strange frisson of recognition. How could she know this woman who stood beside her radiating power and love?

She felt Ms. Sayed's power and strength and as she did the darkness drew back. It tried again but Ms. Sayed shut her eyes and visualised the spheres. She took Scarlett's hand and placed Scarlet's fingers over the shapes. Scarlett felt the shapes shimmer and the darkness retreat slightly. She struggled against it but it would not give up. A hidden memory was forced into her mind.

It was Scarlett's first day at school and the first time she had worn her new school uniform. She had been looking forward to going to **school for it** released **her** from her mother and enabled her to escape her two brothers.

They had been shown around the school and she had felt almost happy as she saw the older kids playing on the swings and imagined herself swinging confidently with a new found friend as they flew up and up until the sky itself would greet them.

Recess time came and she went to the swings but quickly realised that this was not for the preps. She knew, even then how to be patient.

She waited until the bell rang and as the children went to class she grabbed the swing and was soon flying. Time stopped. She was beyond time an eternal pendulum as she swung to her own rhythm.

A teacher had come out and tried to coach her down but she was loving her freedom. Why should she go now, surely a few more minutes wouldn't make any difference?

'You need to come in Scarlett. The other children have started drawing their favourite animal and these are going onto your special trays. Won't that be fun?'

It sounded rather dull to Scarlett. She could draw at home. She wasn't going to mutely give up the joy of the rhythm of swinging **and watching** the sky as it greeted her whilst the sun winked at her as she flew towards it.

'Scarlet? Did you hear me? You must come in. When your start school you have to go to class when you're supposed to. The playground is for recess and lunch breaks.'

Again Scarlett ignored her. She pushed her legs against the pine chips and was once again caught in the sheer pleasure of her rhythm. She could, she thought, go on forever.

'Scarlett! I have tried to be understanding but we can't have children ignoring the teachers. Come down at once!' Scarlett continued swinging and had added to the fun by chanting out a little song that she had made up.

After nearly half an hour she decided that she had had enough. She eased herself of the polished seat and made her way to the exasperated teacher. They went to Scarlett's class and the teacher holding Scarlett's hand as if she might dash off any second.

'I think we're going to have to keep a close eye on Scarlett. She's totally ignored me,' the teacher said as she led Scarlett to her empty seat. Scarlett, however didn't like where she'd been sat. She had wanted to sit at the front of the class but now she was in the back row in a desk by herself.

'I don't want this seat. I'm supposed to sit at the front.'

'If you had come in when you were supposed to,' said her home class teacher, 'you would have been able to sit at the front. But when your seat was empty Zara said that she needed to be closer to the whiteboard so I had to swap seats. I'm sure you'll soon get used to it.'

'No I won't. I waited and waited for my turn on the swing and the big kids wouldn't get off. It's their fault, not mine.' She had sulked for the rest of the day and had sat staring out of the window and refused to sit on the mat in front of the teacher when it was story time.

Thus, Scarlett's first day had branded her 'uncooperative' and as Scarlett soon discovered there wasn't a lot they could do to change her behaviour. Time out? Who cared? As long as she could draw she was happy and the teachers had called in the special education teacher, thinking that perhaps, Scarlett needed one on one attention. It was a sound strategy but Scarlett by now was relishing being an outsider. It gave her the freedom she wanted and besides she could read anyway. She was from time to time disappointed that she wasn't part of the group but it was a feeling that didn't last long.

Soon she began to be taunted by her classmates but she was immune to what they said. This had worked well except for the day when **Zachary** the brightest boy in her class decided to try to exploit her one weakness **which was her mother**. **Zachary's** mother knew Scarlett's mother and Zach had his ammunition ready to fire.

It was just after the lunch bell went and Zach, with a gaggle of his mates, swaggered up to Scarlett and stood a few centimetres from her face and **hissed at her**. 'Your mothers a cripple and my mum said that she looks like an old witch.' He grabbed a broom and threw it against her chest. 'Hop on that and fly home.' He beamed with his perceived wit and the group of children gathered around them waited enthralled.

Their wait was a short one. Scarlett took the broom and attacked him beating him over his shoulders and head. He tired to duck but, she was indeed, in this moment a **daemon**. She continued to thrash him and he fled amidst the astonished looks of his once admirers.

For the next three years she followed her own curriculum but then one day she decided it was now time to see what it was like in the class. She was ignored but she was bright and her reputation meant that none of the students dared go near her. She was a satellite orbiting their collective sun and though at times she wished she had at least one friend she carried on happy enough with the way things were.

The memory faded and she felt the power that was astonishingly coming from Ms.Sayed. Black against white. Darkness against shadow. Ms. Sayed had managed to reignite the power that Scarlett had felt when she had defeated **Zachary**. It was enough. The darkness left her and Ms. Sayed took her hand away from Scarlet and stood next to her.

Scarlett was covered in perspiration and she looked at Ms. Sayed who nodded and Scarlett left the room. As she did Ms.Sayed was once more an ordinary teacher continuing with her lesson as if nothing had happened.

Scarlett left and she quickly walked to the bus stop. When she arrived there was a raucous group of boys she knew from her school. They had skipped class and hung around in a rowdy group smoking and laughing.

She hesitated for a moment and decided she couldn't deal with their taunts which she knew would be forthcoming. She stepped off the footpath but her hesitation had signalled her vulnerability. The elder of the rowdy gaggle stood in front of her and blocked her path.

'How come a dork like you is skipping school?'

'Perhaps I was looking for another dork and it looks like I got lucky.' He grinned admiring her sarcasm.

'I've heard you've got a bit of a reputation.'

'Have I indeed?'

'Fiery, was the word most often used by the Plebs.'

'I thought that you were supposed to be dumb? Didn't you fail every subject including woodwork?

'A proud record. I was especially pleased that I failed woodwork. Apparently I was the first student **not** to pass. Even poor old Mr Grundy couldn't pretend that what I made looked anything like it was supposed to. When he picked it up it fell apart. So I'm dumb and you're smart. Perhaps we should hook up?'

'Sound like you're trying to catch a fish,' she joked and because for some inexplicable reason she wanted to make him laugh, she ran off laughing and ran across the road. 'Look out!' Darcy yelled. She looked up and saw the truck. It was trying to stop and the sound of its brakes rattled her head but she was unable to move. She saw someone running and then she was flung aside by Darcy and the truck swerved missing them both by a few centimetres.

She'd knocked her head on the ground and felt dizzy and shocked. The Driver jumped out of his cab and ran up to them.

'What in God's **name** are you two playing at? You're lucky you're not dead. The pair of you are idiots. Was this some stupid version of playing chicken?' he waited but they said nothing. He shook his head and climbed back into the truck and Drove off.

'Are you okay' asked Darcy as he slowly got to his feet. His face was bleeding and he had a long gravel rash along his arm that oozed blood onto the white gravel that sat at the edge of the road.

'I think so,' Scarlett said but her foot hurt and her head felt like it was going to burst.

'You look like shit,' Darcy said carefully helping her to her feet.

'Thanks. So, do you.'

'My foot feels like I've sprained something and my head hurts but I could have been . . .'

'Killed is the word I think you're looking for', said Darcy. She looked at him and for the first time looked into his eyes. They were as round and innocent as a child's. 'I think they're called baby blue,' he said fluttering his long, black eyelashes at her and grinning like he had won the lottery.

'I might be in the papers tomorrow. I can see the headlines now: 'Brave hero saves girlfriend from out of control truck.'

'Girlfriend?'

'Yes, you're a girl, aren't you? Now that I've saved your life you have to be my friend. That's in all the books on chivalry.'

'How come you act like you know nothing when you're at school? I don't get it.'

'It's a game I play.'

'But why?'

'I think schools are a waste of time. Once you're past primary school if you have any sense at all you can teach yourself. Books, Google and lots of time finding out about things that really interest you. It makes you self reliant and you're better prepared for going to uni. Not that I'm going there. I'm off to see the world in my luxury yacht.'

'I can guess its name.'

'Can you indeed?

'Delusional, that's the perfect name for your boat. You can design your own flag. That'll keep you busy for the next few years.' He laughed but said nothing but she saw that in spite of his bravado she had hurt his feelings. 'I'm sorry. I was trying to be funny but it came out as if I was being mean.' He looked embarrassed and she shocked herself by kissing him on the cheek.

'Now that's what I call magic. One kiss and all of my delusions and troubles disappear.'

'I wish something would get rid of my headache as easily as that. It's really starting to hurt and I'm getting dizzier.'

'You may have concussion. Is it called delayed concussion? I've forgotten even though I've done the first aid certificate. You should go to hospital and get checked out. It could be serious.'

'I'll be fine.'

'You need to get it checked out. Come on. My car is parked around the corner. You stay here and I'll be back.' She wanted to object and felt foolish and if she was being weak but she knew that he was right. He ran down the side street and Drove back and helped her into the car.

'Let me know if you're going to puke.' She tried to think of a comeback but she was now feeling really sick and she began to get worried. He was right, she thought and what if it was something serious?'

'It could be serious,' he said as if he had read her mind, 'I've heard of cases . . .'

'Darcy please. Just be quiet and Drive. I'll let you know if I'm going to be sick.'

He pulled out into the traffic and twenty minutes later they arrived at the hospital. He tried to find a car park but couldn't so he parked illegally and she was too tired to object. All she wanted to do was sleep. She forced herself to keep herself awake and at last she was in a small room waiting to see a doctor. Darcy was unsure if he was allowed to go into Scarlett's room but he went in and saw that Scarlett was asleep. Her long red hair cascaded around her face making her look like a heroine from a children's picture book.

He sat down on the chair near the bed and looked out of the window. He could see the trees outside and was pleased that she would see them when she woke.

He watched the leaves as they moved in the breeze and in spite of his worry about Scarlett he was strangely at peace. He had never spoken to her before yet he felt as if they had known each other for a long time. He loved her sense of humour and her repartee and the fact that, like him, she was something of an outsider.

He saw how lovely she was but unexpectedly, he now felt more as if he were her brother and not a potential boyfriend. He couldn't understand what had changed but he knew that it had and though he was disappointed he knew that it was meant to be.

He heard her moan and he got up and stood next to her not knowing what to do. Should he say something or simply let her be? As he stood there she began to move her head from side to side as if she were having a nightmare. She opened her eyes but they were staring into the distance and were seeing something that he could not.

Although he knew that there was nothing there he suddenly shivered and felt the room grow cold. And was he imagining it, or had the room, in spite of the brightness of the lights **grown** dimmer?

It was as if there was something or someone in the room. Someone who had robbed the room of its life. No sooner had he thought this when the lights went out and he could no longer hear the background noises of the hospital. Gone were the sounds of trolleys being pushed along, gone were the voices that had been so evident a few seconds ago, gone too, it seemed was the very building itself.

He felt his shivering grow more intense and soon he was shaking as if he were in an icy storm lost on the tundra in the wilderness. This was a place of emptiness, a void, a chasm of nothingness that reduced his humanity each second as he stood with his arms now wrapped around him to try to keep some of his body **heat** from dissipating. He knew that he was in danger but from what and how?

He had of course experienced fear before. The fear of his father's rage and he beatings he got when he tried to protect his little sister when his father mocked her backwardness and his mother, mouse timid, fled from the kitchen into the garden where she could not hear his screams. She always took refuge amongst the tangled beauty of her precious flowers that would be trampled into the ground by her husband when he was in one of his rages.

He had never thought that anything could be worse than what he'd experienced during those Dreadful years until his father one night, apocalyptic with fury had had a stroke. He fell to the floor with a look of astonishment on his face that seemed to last too long as Darcy watched him dying.

He made no effort to help even as his father tried to speak. He'd been dead to Darcy for as long as he could remember. He felt as much pity as one would if he were a fly that had suddenly collapsed after bashing itself against the mocking panes of glass promising a freedom that would never come.

He forced himself to stop thinking of what his father was like and what he had done. Was Scarlett having a nightmare or could she too feel the change in the room? He touched her on the shoulder and whispered her name.

At first she didn't react but as he repeated her name she opened her eyes and tried to get out of bed. 'Hey! You can't get out of bed yet. Look at you. You're a mess.'

'Thanks Darcy. A few kind words are what I need not to be told that I look like crap.'

'I never used that word. I said mess. There's a big difference.'

'Well let's not debate it right now. I need to get out of here. There's something wrong with this room. I know that sounds odd but I can feel it.'

'I did too! It was like . . .'

'Something was trying to eat your soul.'

'Shit Scarlett. A nice turn of phrase but not something I wanted to hear.'

'You felt it too. I know you did. I can tell by your face. You look like you've seen the proverbial ghost.'

'So what are we going to do?'

'We're leaving,' Scarlett said as she climbed out of bed. 'I'm not staying here for another minute. I might need to lean on you but I'm sure you won't mind being all strong and tough for a few minutes will you?' She smiled at him. It was a wan and feeble smile and she too was shivering but she was determined to leave.

'Which way are the lifts?'

'They're just a few rooms away,' said Darcy.' Soon we'll be out of here.' She said nothing but she found herself leaning more heavily on Darcy than she thought she would and resented that she felt so weak. She wanted to go faster. If a nurse came in that would be it. She knew that she'd be **escorted back to her room**. 'Hurry up! Darcy. 'We're going too slowly.'

'Said the tortoise to the rabbit.'

'Please Darcy. No jokes. I have to feel the fresh air on my face and feel free. I felt I was trapped in there. I don't want to experience anything like that ever again.'

'Fine by me.' They reached the lifts and Darcy pushed the button and Scarlett was pleased to see that the lift had only one floor to go before it reached them. The doors opened and a doctor and nurse came out and saw that she was obviously unwell.

'Wait miss. You don't look well enough to be leaving. Have you been discharged because if you have it's too soon?

'I'm fine thanks. Just a bit weak. They said I could go.'

'Really? Who was the doctor who discharged you?'

'I'm not sure. He was in such a hurry I didn't catch his name.'

'What about your friend here? Do you remember the doctor's name?'

'No. Sorry. I was so relieved that Scarlett could go I didn't really listen.'

'There's something not right here,' said the doctor as the nurse looked on suspiciously. 'I think I just call downstairs and make sure that everything's in order. If you would take a seat I give them a call and we can get this sorted out.'

'But we were discharged!' Scarlett said thing as she tried to walk out. The nurse blocked her way and Scarlett leant over and whispered in Darcy's ear. 'We have to get away.' Darcy pushed the button of the lift and the doors closed. The nurse tried to put her hand between the door and the gap but she was too slow. Soon they were on the ground floor and out through the glass doors.

'Now what?' asked Darcy.

'I suppose you'd better take me home but to be honest I don't feel up to dealing with my mum or my brothers.'

'Problems?'

'Mum's been sick for ages. It's degenerative and so she's getting worse. Fletcher and Elliot are useless and when they're not fighting they're on the internet. So I have to do nearly everything. Mum tries but she won't accept help from a carer and the boys are useless so I'm the one who's stuck.'

'Can't you convince her to get a carer? It's not fair on you. Can't she understand that?'

Scarlett sighed. How she wished her mother would understand but Scarlett was cursed by her own efficiency. She hid her feelings and tiredness as she went about the house cleaning and doing the cooking. Fletcher and Elliot seemed not to have any qualms about not doing anything. Too often Scarlett had raged at their selfishness but they ignored her and locked themselves into their bedrooms where they'd installed their own locks. 'We need our privacy,' they had said when Scarlett asked why but she knew the reason even before she asked it.

She yearned to escape. She loved her mother but with the shopping and school and everything else all she had by means of an escape were her precious circles.

She noticed Darcy looking at her and she saw how concerned he was. She was not used to kindness and wanted to lean on him, just for a few seconds, but she stopped herself. She had to remain strong even if she felt unwell.

'Come back to my joint for a few hours. I'll make you something to eat and get you a coffee. I've even got my own coffee making machine. I'm quite the barista.'

She wanted to say yes but knew that it wasn't possible. Her mother would be worried at her being late and any stress made her condition worse.

'Thanks Darcy but as much as I'd love to have a coffee made with your expert skills I have to get home.'

'So I'll Drive you home and you can ask me in and I'll make you a coffee at your place.'

She wanted to resist but as she saw his face and his look of expectancy she surprised herself. 'Thanks Darcy. It's a deal. Unfortunately we don't have a coffee machine. It's a bit beyond our budget and I won't Drink instant coffee but you can make me a cup of tea.'

'You'll ruin my reputation but it's a deal.' He put the car into gear and they pulled out of the hospital car park. 'Which way?'

'Left. **Then** get onto Freeman Road. I'll direct you from there.'

'Freeman Road?'

'It goes out to the Western suburbs. It's a crap suburb but with rents being so high it's all mum can afford.'

'It can't be worse than my place and I bet it's a lot bigger.'

'Bigger? You've got to be kidding! Our house only has **three tiny bedrooms** and a **minute** lounge **room** and even smaller kitchen. Needless to say I have to sleep on the couch. I hate it.'

'Still bigger that mine.'

'So are you about to tell me that you live in a cardboard box and inside this box is your coffee machine?'

'Not quite. It's a caravan. It's really cool. It's perfect for me.'

'You live by yourself?'

'Yep. Suits me down to the ground. No hassles. I can come and go when I please and the rent is cheap as.'

'Sounds great. All that peace.'

'I'm prepared to share.'

'With me?'

'No with an elephant.'

'I'll bring my trunk.' He looked at her and burst out laughing. 'You're great. You feel like shit and you can still crack jokes. You've got a crappy deal at home but you still get to school and do all that other stuff. I think you're amazing.'

She felt herself blush but was delighted with what he'd said. How, she wondered could she have been so wrong about someone? 'Thank you.'

'It's true. Now which way?'

They followed the road and passed by old factories and run down business, many of which had been boarded up. The walls and fences were covered in graffiti and smog from the factories had covered the buildings making them look bleak.

'Next on the left,' Scarlett said embarrassed that Darcy was about to see her house. He turned the car and travelled a few hundred metres when she told him to stop.

'This is it. Tres joli it is not.'

'I don't speak Spanish.'

'It's French but it probably sounds like Spanish. My French teacher says I have a lousy accent.'

'Not to me you don't.' This time she stopped herself from blushing but quickly got out of the car and waited for him to get out. He stepped out and she saw that he was surprised. The house was small and run down but someone had made the front garden which bloomed with colour.'

'I bet you did this.'

'Therapy. I take cuttings and somehow they seem to just grow. They're plants that are easy to grow. Daises, geraniums and whatever I can pinch from people's gardens. My favourite is that rose.'

'The one with the three different colours in it?'

'Yep. It starts off red then fades to orange and finally a kind a purple. I grew it from a cutting. Anyway that's enough about my little garden come in.' As they were about to go in a white car pulled up.

They turned around and Scarlett was surprised to see Ms. Sayed climb out of her car.

'Looks like someone's in trouble,' commented Darcy as Ms. Sayed headed towards them.

'I can't believe she's come here,' said Scarlett. She's not the type. What Scarlett didn't tell Darcy was how Ms. Sayed had responded to Scarlett earlier that afternoon. It would sound absurd.

'Why come on the day before holidays?' Darcy asked looking at Scarlett as somehow she would naturally know the answer. 'I don't know.' But she did. She tried to look relaxed but knew she was deceiving no one including herself. As Ms.Sayed came closer she saw at once that she was not the school teacher she had known. Again she had morphed into whatever it was that she had changed into earlier.

'I know it's been two years since I had her for a teacher but she never looked like that when I was in her class. What's going on?' he asked. Scarlett looked at him and saw how surprised he was. She shrugged and then before she could say anything Ms. Sayed was standing in the front garden admiring the plants as if it was the most natural thing in the world for her to be doing.

'I like you're little front garden Scarlett. Colour is so important don't you think? It chases away the cobwebs from our minds.'

'**Thank** you Ms. Sayed. Is there something wrong? Have Fletcher and Elliot been expelled or something?'

'No Scarlett nothing like that. Though I do admit they can be challenging at times.'

'All of the time actually. But if you're not here for that is it me? Have I done something wrong?'

'Scarlett I'm not the school police but I do need to talk to you and to Darcy as well.'

'Me? Asked Darcy astonished. Why would she want to speak to him? He hadn't been at the school for two years. 'But I don't go to school anymore Ms. Sayed. I left in year eleven.'

'I'm well aware of when you left Darcy. It was a shame. You have such a great mind only you never used it.'

'Then . . .'

'Then Darcy, perhaps with Scarlett's permission, we can go inside. I have something very important to say to both of you. You're going to struggle to believe me but let's go inside shall we?'

Scarlett hoped that her mother was in bed. This was a conversation that she knew was somehow going to change her life and she felt too nervous to say anything. She opened the door and led them into the cramped lounge room with its battered furniture which sat forlornly on a faded carpet whose colour had been drained out of it years before.

'Please sit down,' Scarlett said as she brushed uselessly at the hairs that their Jack Russel dog had left behind. 'Jasper's not supposed to sit on the furniture but I'm the only one who seems to mind, so he does what he likes.'

'I've sat in places less comfortable than this Scarlett. A few dog hairs aren't going to worry me.'

'Can I get you a cup of coffee or tea or some water?'

'I'd prefer a large gin and tonic but I'll settle for a cup of tea. Thanks.'

'A G and T? I didn't think you'd be the type to Drink alcohol Ms. Sayed.'

'And why would that be Darcy? I suppose you had me pigeon holed as an old maid who had a tipple or two of a sherry when I was feeling particularly adventurous? No doubt, in your mind, I **have an** old cat sitting on my lap or lying next to my knitting basket where I made tea cosies for the older members of our community. Was that the picture you had young man?'

'No I . . .'

'Sometimes Darcy it's best to say nothing. You'll try to deny it but we both know that you'd be prevaricating wouldn't we?'

'I'm not sure.'

'Is that because you don't know what prevaricating means or because I was right.'

'One of the above Ms. Sayed.'

'A wise response Darcy. Now where's that tea I've been promised?'

Just then Scarlett came in with three mugs of tea on a wooden tray. She had managed to find a jug with only one small crack in it and had smelt the milk to see if it was still okay. A small sugar bowl sat in the middle of the tray and its colours reflected those of the garden.

'What a lovely little jug Scarlett. I believe it was your grandmother's?'

'Yes,' said Scarlett startled. 'But how could you know that? I don't understand.'

'You will. Let me show off a bit more if I may. Her name was Rose and her husband's name was James. They were English and came from Kent. He used to work in wood. Making handmade furniture if I remember correctly. I can get a bit confused from time to time.'

Scarlett and Darcy looked at each other. Darcy raised his eyebrows as if asking Scarlett if what they had heard was true. She saw his astonished expression and she knew that it reflected her own. This was not possible. What had happened in the class room was unbelievable enough but this?

Scarlett tried to take a sip of her tea but it went down the wrong way and she started coughing and to her embarrassment she couldn't stop. At last, after the last paroxysm, she sniffed and looked at Ms. Sayed waiting for an explanation.

Ms. Sayed gazed back at her as unreadable as an owl and merely sat there waiting for Scarlett to speak. Scarlett looked back at her. She realised that she had never really looked at her before. Of course she had seen her face, knew some of her mannerism and her voice. But as she studied her face more closely she saw that Ms. Sayed was not the slightly vague, albeit, pedantic teacher that Scarlett thought she was.

She saw a middle aged woman whose eyes were green not blue as she had always believed. Her nose was small and was in perfect proportion to the size of her face which was slightly rounded and her face was a mixture of worry lines and laugher lines. In short, it was a face that had seen a great deal. Her wrinkles now seemed as if they were a map, which for the first time Scarlett was studying.

Ms. Sayed sat as if she was unaware of the scrutiny that Scarlett was subjecting her to. She looked as if she were alone in her room idly looking out of the window her mind apparently unoccupied and tranquil. But the longer Scarlett looked the more that she learned.

This woman had known sorrow and pain, and had laughter lines arranged neatly around her mouth, but the overall impression was the one that Scarlett had **seen** in the classroom earlier that day. **Her face was one which reflected** wisdom, kindness and concern.

'I think you've worked me out, at least to some extent Scarlett although your friend Darcy was more interested in looking at you. You are meant to be friends and your friendship will be put to a great test that you may, or may not overcome. You need each other and must learn to trust each other totally. If you don't you will fail and the world will suffer.'

She paused but Scarlett and Darcy were incapable of responding. Were these the deranged mutterings of a deluded woman who hitherto had seemed normal to the point of tediousness and if not what did that mean?

'I see that I have surprised you. Perhaps shocked you a little but there's more. A great deal more that you need to know. I see Scarlett that you're worried that your brothers will burst in any second but they are at the skate park and will stay there until I leave. I know this may be hard for you to believe but it is true.

Now, to the most important part of my reason for being here. I want you to listen and put aside what you consider to be normal or abnormal. It's best if you let me finish what I need to tell you and then you may ask whatever questions you want. I'll tell you the truth no matter what the question, as is the truth of what you are about to hear.'

She looked at them and felt for them. Their world and their beliefs would be changed forever. It was she who had to tell them of their destiny. 'Soon you are going to meet two people, who, like you, are special. Their names are Zerach and Thomas who is his spiritual twin. He also looks exactly like him but you'll see that for yourself in a few days.'

'A few days? How can you . . .'

'Darcy I understand your curiosity but you must wait until I'm finished. The four of you make up the perfect four. Zerach is the most gifted and has the most power. As yet he is unaware of how much power he has. It will come to him when he needs it, but like you will all suffer in the battle that you will face.

Your enemy has no name; but is enormously powerful. It has existed before the universe came into being. I can't reveal too much to you as part of your journey is to discover for yourselves what you will face.

In the **past** there have been a few others who had your gift but they've been crushed by their opponents. You may lose the battle and if you do you too will be destroyed. Each of you has felt the creature as it as it crept into your minds and souls and showed you the nature of its darkness. It can only have this affect on the four of you. You will need courage, love, belief and above all, the ability for you all to stay connected at all times. Once the battle starts, if even one of you let's any of the others down you will place yourselves in grave danger. You may not even survive.'

She leant back in her chair and looked suddenly exhausted. 'You may ask me what questions you have now. But my answers must be brief. It is hard for me to maintain my present state of consciousness for long periods of time.'

'The four of you will need to travel and will not be home for some time. I will be looking after your mother and your brothers. I will change my appearance and the boys will not know me. Your mother will believe that I am her sister. She had a sister once but she died a long time ago. I will make your mother believe that her sister never died and that I am her to look after her. Her sister was called Meg. I will be Meg. It will be hard to maintain my altered appearance but Reuben and Sophia will help me. I must endure what I must endure until the battle is lost or won.'

Scarlett could not process what she was hearing. This woman

must be insane but she knew that her Aunt Meg had died and she knew that her mother and Meg had been exceptionally close. She would wait until Ms. Sayed met her mother. Then if her mother believed that Ms. Sayed was her sister she would be convinced.

'When will you meet mum?' Scarlett asked.

'Tomorrow. I'll be here at three o'clock. School will have finished and Fletcher and Elliot will come straight home after school.'

'But they never come home then! They stay out until it suits them.'

'Scarlett, they will be here. It will be the first sign for you that I'm not insane. If I were, how could I predict what will happen?'

Scarlett knew that she should ask more questions. Dozens but her mind was in a fugue and she sat silently waiting for Darcy to say something. Surely he would ask the questions that she should be asking? She looked at him but for once his animation had deserted him.

'Well if neither of you has any more questions I'll be going. I'll be here at three exactly. I look forward to seeing your mother Scarlett. There is so much that you don't know about her. In time you will learn her story but that, for now will have to wait.'

She got up from her chair and looked at them both and smiled. 'Until tomorrow.'

***

The school bell rang and the students delirious with their sense of freedom cascaded out of the school. Scarlett could not wait to get home. Soon she would know. She saw Darcy waiting for her as he stood next to his car. He waved and she ran over and gave him a quick kiss. 'We'll soon know one way or another.'

'Yep, and my money is on Ms. Sayed being a tad crazy.'

'We'll know in thirty minutes. I can't believe how long today has seemed. All I could think about was what Ms. Sayed said.'

Scarlett didn't know if she wanted it to be true or not. She had after all seen how Ms. Sayed had changed in the classroom whereas Darcy hadn't. She didn't really believe it but nevertheless part of her was afraid. What if it was true? What was the darkness and what powers did it have? She forced herself to stop thinking and looked at the buildings as they slid past the car, their grim ugliness seemed ubiquitous and never ending.

At last they arrived at Scarlett's house. She was surprised to see that her mother was out of bed and sitting in the lounge room. She smiled, and then seeing Darcy, she gave a little half wave as if not knowing what to say.

'Hi mum. This is Darcy. He's a friend of mine. It's great to see you out of bed.'

'I feel a little better today. It's as if I'm expecting another visitor, someone special. I know that must sound silly to you Darcy.'

'Not at all. I'm pleased to meet you. I can see now where Scarlett got her red hair from.'

'We're Irish. A lot of my family had red hair especially Meg. Her hair was like a wild halo. It reminded me on the sun.' They heard of Fletcher and Elliot arguing as they came through the front gate. Scarlett looked at Darcy as if to say 'see this is what they're like.

'What a nice surprise to have you all here together for a change,' said Scarlett's mother. 'I can't remember the last time this happened so soon after school.' She had just finished talking when there was a knock at the door.

'Goodness me. Everything's happening at once. Whoever can that be?'

Scarlett opened the door. A tall woman with bright red hair and freckles stood in front of her. She was dressed in a fashionable pair of jeans and green top. On her back was a large backpack. Her eyes were blue and she looked so much like her mother Scarlett stood there for a moment unable to speak.

'For heaven's sake Scarlett. Ask the person in. We can't have someone standing on the doorstep kept waiting.'

The woman walked in and went up to Scarlett's mother. 'Hi Bridget. I thought I give you a surprise and stay for a while. I'm sick of travelling all around the world and I need to see my sister again. She bent down and hugged Bridgett and gave her a kiss on the cheek.

'Meg! Meg! My God. How long has it been? I can't believe it. You're here at last. You've been travelling for years and now your back.'

'And if you don't mind, I'll be staying for a while. It might be quite a while. But what's happened to you? You don't look like your old self at all. Have you been unwell?'

'I've got this disease thing. I can't even remember what it's called. They want to give me a carer but I'll have no stranger looking after me.'

'Well there's no need now. I'm here and I'll take care of everything. And that means you two as well,' she said glancing at Fletcher and Elliot. 'I won't stand for any nonsense but I'm sure you'll prove yourselves to be fine young men.'

Scarlett looked at Darcy and he looked back. There was nothing to say. What Ms.Sayed had said was true. Scarlett couldn't believe what was happening. Somehow Ms.Sayed had transformed herself into her mother's sister and she felt both astonished and deadly afraid of what was happening.

CHAPTER TWENTY THREE

Zerach

He must find a way to get out of the hospital but how? He left his room and went to the nurses' station and pretended to read one of the notices that were on the wall advertising various help groups that existed after one was discharged. He needed to find a way that he could get past the station without drawing attention to himself.

He stayed for several minutes to ascertain how vigilant the staff was and how hard it would be to go past them. There were three staff. One seemed be on the phone most of the time, another one was answering the various bells that rang. The last one stood there casually talking to visitors but whose eyes didn't seem to miss a thing.

Zerach knew that he wouldn't be able to stroll past him. He had a brief fantasy of disguising himself but he knew that he was deluding himself. Disguise himself as who, and more to the point, with what?

As he turned away he heard Dr Michal. Heard her fake concern and kind tones that he knew hid her poison. 'Zerach,' she said as if she'd stumbled upon him by accident. 'It's good to see you up and about. I've spoken to the duty psychiatrist and she agreed that we can spend some time together. Only for a half an hour though. She was quite strict about that. A bit like me I suppose. There's a consulting room we can use. We were fortunate because usually it's booked out but there was a cancellation so now we can have it.

'It's this way Zerach. Just down the corridor.' She opened the door to the consulting room which, unlike her own office was alive and bright with colour. A Manet, a Monet and other French impressionists hung on the walls and he felt soothed by their beauty and the genius of the artists.

'I see you like the paintings Zerach. Why's that?'

'Because they're nothing like the one you've got in your office with its three crows. You have to know it's sinister. How come you put up paintings like that when your patients aren't well? I don't get it.'

'Oh, but you do Zerach. You get it perfectly. You instinctively understood what it meant. As for my other patients, well let me share a little secret with you. I only have a few very special patients.'

'Special? What do you mean?'

'I think we can stop pretending, now don't you?'

'Pretending? Pretending what?'

'You never were a good liar Zerach. None of your kind are. You once called me a witch. Do you remember that?'

'I did and you are. There's something wrong with you.'

'On the contrary the opposite is true. I'm not a witch but like you I have powers and mine are far more developed than yours. You keep on seeing the spheres and I told you that you were a schizophrenic. You and I both know that's not true. Events are happening quicker than I thought. That did surprise me.'

'But why are you telling me this now? Why take the risk?'

'Risk? Risk? You are an infant in a young man's body. What risks did you think I was exposing myself to?'

'You know exactly what I mean. I'll tell people. I'll tell mum and dad and every person that I meet or see or know **claiming that I had schizophrenia when I don't**. You'll be stuffed.'

'An amusing colloquial expression but on the contrary it will be you who'll be "stuffed" as you so inelegantly put it.'

'Why's that?'

'Have a wee think about it. What have you been diagnosed with?'

'You know so why ask?'

'Humour me just for a moment.'

'A schizophrenic,' he whispered.

'Exactly. If and when you tell people about this imagined conversation what are they going to think? You're not stupid Zerach so don't bother to answer.'

He knew she was right. If he said anything they would assume that he was experiencing a schizophrenic episode. He had been diagnosed. He had been treated. He had been on anti-psychotic meds and the duty psychiatrists had confirmed Dr Michal's diagnosis.

'Now who has the upper hand?'

'I still may if . . . if . . .'

'If you find the others is the point you're trying to get to. Always so circumspect. Just get to the point Zerach. I'm a busy professional who has to go and consult with the duty psychiatrist about your latest fantasy. It should make for interesting reading. Would you like a few key words for you to understand how much power I have over you Zerach? Permit me to give you a small sample'

'Quote: "In spite of ongoing treatments over the last year Zerach continues to experience ongoing and persistent fantasies that are not, unfortunately responding to conventional medication. I suggest a review of his treatment, and given his latest delusional episode, it's my considered opinion that he would be more amenable to treatment in a closed psychiatric ward where he can **be better** supervised by staff and other appropriate professionals." How does that sound?'

'You can't do that!'

'Not only can I but in a few minutes of I'm off to make my report and to consult with my colleague. Naturally I'll have to add that in addition to your delusions, you're becoming violent and unpredictable. That will make a nice little addendum don't you think?'

He leapt out of his chair and felt the urge to grab her around her throat. He stopped himself and, suddenly defeated collapsed onto his chair. She smiled pushed her own fingers viciously around her throat and squeezed. She continued for a few more seconds to make sure that it would result in serious bruising then pushed a button under the desk. He heard the alarm sound and three psychiatric nurses ran in.

'He needs to be restrained. He attacked me.' She went to him and put her hand on his arm. 'I'm so sorry this happened Zerach. But with time, and specialised care you will improve. Trust me.'

One of the trio looked at him pityingly and the other smiled. It was a smiled of victory. 'She's a liar; a liar! She strangled herself to make it . . .'

He felt strong arms guide him back, and, as he looked he saw Dr Michal's fake concern before she turned away and smiled.

CHAPTER TWENTY FOUR

The three nurses put him back into his bed. One remained. He was the one who'd smiled at Zerach and he stood there like a prison guard and looked down at Zerach with contempt.

Zerach noticed that his eyes were the same as Dr Michal's. They, like hers missed nothing. He could feel himself being analysed with the same dispassionate, clinical look that was identical to Dr Michal's.

'That went well didn't it? It looks as if we're going to have your company for quite a while. If you behave like that again you could be sectioned for your own safety and that, believe me, creates the ideal situation for Dr Michal and for me as well.'

'You've got nowhere to hide in here. Every move that you make will be scrutinised. Everything noted down and discussed between Dr Michal and your new consulting therapist. Oh, and by the way, if you harbour the slightest hope of trying to get out of here I'd give up on it now. It'll save you a lot of time and trouble. So you may have discovered who you're twin is but it seems to have created more problems than you had before. That's fate for you I suppose.' He laughed and left as he retreated to the office.

Zerach felt defeated. Where were his spheres and why weren't they helping him? He'd not dreamt of them for weeks and had not heard them whisper to him telling him how special he was. How could he be special locked inside a psychiatric ward without any chance of escape?

He wondered if his parents would be able to visit him. What if Dr Michal's report meant that his right to have visitors would be cancelled? He had to speak to them. **He needed to** tell them what was happening but he knew that it would only reinforce their belief that he was still mentally unwell.

She was right. They, along with everyone else would think he was getting worse. He was both psychically trapped and psychologically trapped as well. He Drew his knees up to his chest and gave in to his feelings of despair.

The hours were long. He could hear the clock on the wall its maddening sound reminding him of his status of a prisoner. At last it was meal time, and although he loathed the food he was glad of the interruption as he heard the trolleys being wheeled into the room. He sat up and waited. The nurse placed the trays in front of the other patients and then came up to Zerach.

'Time for your last meal here,' he said.

'Pardon?'

'I said its time for your last meal here. Don't look so worried. You're not off to the guillotine. This isn't the prisoner's last meal request because if it was, I'd be damn disappointed. Bangers and mash not exactly high end living is it?'

Zerach looked at the nurse and the nurse gave him a conspiratorial wink. 'Guess who?'

'I know who you are. You're the other nurse.'

'That's me. The nice one,' he paused for a moment and then sat down on the bed next to Zerach.

'I imagine that you feel like shit at the moment. Tell me if I'm wrong.' In spite of himself Zerach smiled and looked at the man's face more closely.

'You look a bit like a man I met once. He was called Reuben but when I tried to find him again I couldn't'

'Sometimes we find people when we least expect to.'

Zerach looked at him more closely. He was young, unlike Reuben and had the bluest eyes he'd ever seen. His face was thin and he had a goatee that made his look a bit like a medieval aesthete. He impressed

Zerach with his aura of kindness and love and most powerfully of all was his aura of wisdom. It was then that Zerach knew who he was. He daren't say it out aloud lest he sounded like a fool but he knew. He knew.

Reuben smiled and leant forward and gave him a hug. 'Hello Zerach. Thought you'd seen the last of me eh?'

'I knew! I knew it was you. But how . . . how . . .'

'It's too hard to explain. You thought that **the** spheres had abandoned you but they never will. In fact they were there at your conception.'

'Yuck, grimaced Zerach I can't think of mum and dad actually doing it. It seems so gross.' Reuben laughed. It was a laugh that seemed to come from a place inside him that like a long unopened door had remained stuck for years.

'Gross? Zerach you made **me** laugh which I haven't done in. . . . well let's just say a long, long time.'

'How long? I want to know more about you.'

'One hundred or perhaps a bit longer? Two hundred years or so? I get confused with time.'

'How come you can live for so long? You're like that guy in the Bible. He was called Methuselah. He was supposed to have lived for nearly a thousand years.'

'Well scholars may disagree with you there but I'm not here to give you a lesson in theology. I'm here for something else.'

'To destroy Dr Michal,' Zerach said with relish. 'She deserves it.'

'My role is not to mete out justice Zerach. In my realm that's not how things work. We're not allowed to harm anyone even if they harm others. It's not our purpose. Our purpose is far, far more important. At the moment my task is to get you out of here to find your twin.'

'I know his name,' Zerach said excitedly. 'His name is Thomas.'

'Yes it is. It means twin but I think that you know that now don't you?'

'Yes and you've know forever.'

'Not quite forever but yes a long time.'

'Can you tell me how long? There's so much I need to know.'

'Not now Zerach. We need to get you out soon. Dr Michal is on her way back and we must hurry.'

'But how can you get me out. There's that nurse over there who looks like an escaped crim and he's starting to look suspicious.'

'Then let's not give him time to get more suspicious shall we? I'll leave you for now but will be back **when the staff changes shifts. Her spy** won't be there but she'll have someone else to take his place. You need to do exactly what I tell you to do.'

'He's coming!'

'I know he is and I'm going. Stay alert.'

'Thought you two were having a party. Chatting away like old friends. You're a nurse in case you've forgotten. You're not here to write his bloody biography.'

'Thank you Jude. I must remember that. You're quite right. I take too long with the patients. I'll make sure that this patient won't be put in that situation again.'

'See that you don't. Don't forget you're the new nurse and I've been here for years. So you need to listen to me.'

'Understood perfectly Jude. It won't happen again. You have my word for it.' He winked at Zerach and placed his pen in his top pocket and went to another patient. A few minutes later Zerach looked around the ward but Reuben was gone but now he was too excited to stay in bed. He got up and young patient in his ward waved to him. He was surprised for all he had seen the young man do was to lie in his bed and not speak. He felt a little nervous but he went over and stood by his bed.

'Hi I'm Zerach,' he said.

'Declan.' He pulled himself into a sitting position and winced with pain. 'Shit. It still bloody hurts. Don't ever try to jumping out of a window when you're trying to top yourself and if you do make sure it's higher that two story's. All I did was broke both of my legs and buggered up a few other bits and pieces.'

'I'm sorry,' said Zerach who was shocked and didn't know what to say. Declan had shaved his head and had scars that ran down his arm like two train lines. 'Junky,' Declan said as he noticed Zerach looking at his arm. 'Apparently the correct approach is to pretend that you haven't seen anything which is bullshit because unless you we're blind or shitfaced you'd had to notice.' He waited for Zerach to answer him but he was, he knew out of his depth. How did he talk to someone his age who'd tried to kill himself?

'Can I ask you something?'

'Ask away. Hang on. I've forgotten your name already. But I do remember it was weird but kind of cool and it started with a Z. So I have to get some credit eh?'

'Zerach. It's a Jewish name.'

'Are you Jewish?'

'Yes.'

'And you go the temple and all that sort of shit and wear those funny little cap things?'

'Yes, well I used to go but we call it a synagogue and the caps are called Kippahs.'

'It sounds like the name of a cat I had once. It used to bite me when I was little. I hated it. Then it got itself run over and I cried. Make sense of that eh?'

'I suppose that we can grieve over animals even though we didn't like them. At least I think we might.'

'Shit you sound like one of those religious guys. Full of wisdom or full of shit. Sometimes I find it hard to tell the difference.'

'If you meet someone who's really wise you'll know it.'

'You're not one of those religious freaks are you? Because I . . .'

'No but I know someone who's wise and there's something special about them. You'll know it if you ever meet one.'

'No shit eh? Well who is this guy who you know? Is he or she running around the place being wise to everyone? 'Cos I'd like to meet him or her and then he can tell me how to get out of this shithole.'

'Did you see the man who was talking to me before?'

'Do you meant the dude with the little goatee thing who also happens to be a nurse? Nope. Saw nothing like that.' Zerach laughed and decided he could trust Declan. In spite of his pain and his past he could still make jokes.'

'Yes smart arse. That guy. Well he's the one who's really wise. He's much more than that but I don't think I'm supposed to talk about that.'

'The great nurse with a goatee mystery eh? The riddle of the winks.'

'How did you see him wink? How can you crack jokes as clever as that and . . . and . . .'

'Aren't clever and funny kids allowed to top themselves?'

'I'm sorry. I don't know what to say or even if I did how to say it.'

'Don't worry. My shrink means well but he doesn't know what to say either but he's nice and he tries. Still, whatever he says or doesn't say, in the end it will amount to jack shit because I can't go home so I'll eventually pretend to be better. Take my medication whilst I'm in here then go back on the streets turning tricks to make money so I can score. Not much to look forward to is it?'

'Turn tricks?'

'You really should have stayed in your safe synagogue. Turning a trick. I thought everyone knew what that meant.'

'If you're saying what I think you're saying you can't. Anything could happen. You're too young.'

'That's how I score with the punters. My good looks. Works every time. Except . . . except . . .'

'Let's just say that I've had the odd punter who's turned out to be a total prick. Sorry, shit pun, but you develop a special sense. Usually it keeps you safe.'

'And what happens when it doesn't?'

'You get the shit kicked out of you and finish up in hospital. Then you go to a half way house which is a boring as hell so I piss off back to the streets.'

'And that's your life and that's why you jumped out of the window.'

'Spot on Sherlock. Pity I'm not Holmes. We'd have made a great team.'

'But we can.'

'What?'

'Make a team. You can stay with us.'

'Stay with you? I don't think your parents would like a junkie rent boy living with them. But thanks Zerach. I'll remember what you said. If I get desperate I'll call you.'

'Really?'

'No not really. You're a nice guy but I think we both know things like that just don't happen. Except on a Disney film or something but in this life, well it's not going to work for me.'

'Please Declan. It would work. Trust me.'

'I trust you. It's the world I don't trust. But thanks. I'll never forget what you've said.'

'Can I give you my mobile number at least let me do that? Then if you ever need help you can ring me.'

Declan said nothing. He looked past Zerach as if he wasn't there and a small, sad smile crossed his face. Shakily he stood up and held out his hand. 'I promise you this much. I won't say yes but I won't say no.'

Although Zerach tried not to look at the clock above the window he couldn't help but notice that the hour was nearly up. He saw that Declan had noticed him looking and looked away but Declan knew that he was waiting and he knew for whom.

CHAPTER TWENTY FIVE

Three o'clock. The door opened and the new staff walked in. For a moment Zerach couldn't see Reuben then he saw him as he walked into the room. As the process of the shift change was occurring Reuben quickly went to Zerach. 'Don't ask questions. Just do what I say and as quickly as you can.' He pulled out a nurse's uniform from under his coat and secretly handed it to Zerach. 'Put it on. It'll only fool them for a second. When I leave follow me.'

'But they'll know! They're not that dumb.'

'No there not but there's going to be a diversion. It'll be chaotic and that's when we move. Ready?'

Zerach felt disappointed. He had expected Reuben to do something otherworldly although what that would have entailed he had no idea. However, simply putting on a nurses uniform was a real let down. Besides what if it didn't work? Why weren't the spheres invading the room and . . . and, what he asked himself. Fly at the nurses, blind them with their lights, crash around the ward as if they were some sort of electrical storm? He knew he was being infantile.

He quickly put on the uniform and even found a security tag and lanyard which he put around his neck. He might be disappointed but Reuben had been thorough. He looked at the photo of himself and the ID card. It looked perfect. Feeling somewhat better he waited.

Reuben was talking to the nurse who'd spoken to him earlier. He was surprised to see that Reuben had made him and the rest of the new shift laugh. As they continued to laugh Reuben came out and nodded.

Zerach knew that he had to look as natural as he could. In spite of the uniform and the blue ribbon and ID around his neck he was not confident. He walked towards the door and stood next to Reuben who was blocking their field of vision. Feeling like an animal about to be shot Zerach went towards the door.

The nurses looked up and as they did there was a huge crashing noise. They all turned to see what was happening. It was Declan. Somehow he had a piece of pipe and he was attacking the window with it.

'You can't keep me here you bastards,' he yelled. The nurses rushed over to him and he and Reuben fled through the doors and down the long corridor. Soon they reached the main lobby area and Rueben gave a casual wave and they walked through the doors. Zerach couldn't believe it. Reuben's dumb plan had actually worked. Reuben led him to his car and they slowly drove away from the hospital.

'How did you know that there was going to be a diversion?'

'Just a lucky guess I suppose.'

'You can't say that! If it wasn't for Declan doing what he did then the whole thing wouldn't have worked. You knew. You knew, so why not tell me?'

'Zerach you may be special but I can't always tell you what you want to know. I'm sorry but that's how it is.'

'But what about Declan? What's going to happen to him? He'll be in there for ages now.'

'And is that such a bad thing?'

'I . . . I . . .'

'Exactly you don't know Zerach. The hospital is not a bad place. They will help him and eventually he'll go to detox. It's better than being on the streets and surviving by having to do the things he did to survive. It would have destroyed him.'

'So you can tell the future?'

'I'm simply common sense. **There's** nothing special about that. **Still he might surprise you one day when you least expect it.'**

'Really?'

'Yes Zerach, really. Now let's go. We can't afford to hang about.'

They drove for a few kilometres and Reuben pulled up outside a large clothing store and stopped the car. 'Here we are,' he said.

'Here we are? Reuben, we're at a shopping centre! I'm supposed to be finding the others and you want to go shopping?' Reuben laughed and tapped him on his shoulder.

'And part of your plan is to get around in a nurses uniform with a fake ID?'

Zerach felt like a fool. He'd needed clothes and he couldn't go home. His parents would call the hospital and Dr Michal and they'd take him back. He had to find Thomas. That was his first and for the moment his only goal.

They climbed out of the car and went into the shop and soon Zerach emerged wearing new clothes and carrying a shopping bag. He also had a new wallet with five hundred dollars in it that Rueben had given him.

'Looks like you're all set then,' said Reuben. 'It's up to you now.'

'You're' leaving me? Here?'

'It has to be somewhere Zerach. For the moment my part is done. Now it's up to you. Find him. Find the other two and stop what still may happen in spite of everything we do to stop it. I know you have lots of questions but there isn't time. The spheres have called you. Answer the call before it's too late. Now go, my friend.'

As he was about to walk off he heard Rueben toot. He ran back thinking that Reuben had changed his mind. He felt both elated and relived. He would have Rueben with him after all. He jumped into the car and waited for them to leave. 'No Zerach You've misunderstood me. I have to go but I forgot to give you this.' He handed Zerach a credit card and told him the pin number. 'You will need money. You can't as yet go back to your parents. When you meet Thomas and the others you'll have to travel. There's as much money in the account as you need.'

'But how can you know how much we might need? It's not possible.'

'You were disappointed when I didn't use what you like to call "magic" when we left the hospital. I think I'm allowed to show off just a little bit. After all it has been nearly three hundred years since I've used that particular gift so this is your little bit of magic.

Whenever you use the card and whatever amount you need it will always be available. Don't ask how. It's too hard to explain. You're going to need more money than you think. The card will only work if you are pursing what you must do. It can't be used for frivolities. I don't expect you would do that but remember there are four of **you** and you're all so young. One of you will be impetuous. So there it is. A magic credit card. Not a bad trick for a man of my age eh?'

Zerach took the card. As he did he felt Reuben's hand brush his? Again he felt Reuben's power and his love. Zerach didn't want to leave but he knew that now it was up to the four of them. He wished he wasn't part of it all but he was The Chosen One. Whether he felt ready or not, **he** was it. He gave Reuben a hug and quickly opened the door and walked away.

He needed to find a bus stop and work out how to get to Thomas's place. Soon he found a bus shelter and he worked out the route. All he had to do was to convince Thomas that four teenagers were supposed to fight against the darkness and that he was the Chosen One.

The big problem was of course that he would sound exactly like a delusional schizophrenic. Thomas would need to be convinced but how?

CHAPTER TWENTY SIX

Zerach and Thomas

The bus stopped and Zerach climbed out. It had taken him two hours to arrive at the correct suburb. He wandered around for half an hour and realised that he had no phone. How much easier he thought would it be if he could use Google maps to find Thomas's house.

He saw a large shopping centre on his left and he walked towards it. It was new and as yet there was no graffiti on the side of the building and the trees that had been used to landscape around it were still young and fresh.

He walked to the glass doors and he felt the cool air greet him and he realised that he was hot, hungry and thirsty. He had no cash and even though Reuben had said that the card would work he was not entirely convinced. It seemed too preposterous, like something out of science fiction movie. Still he had no choice.

He quickly found an ATM machine and gingerly inserted the card. He pressed in the pin number and to his amazement and relief it opened up the account. He had no idea how much money he would need, but mindful of Reuben's warning about using the card prudently he took out fifty dollars. It would be enough for some food and a Drink after which he could purchase a pre-paid mobile.

He gobbled down his lunch and went to the phone shop. He scanned the line of phones and avoided the most expensive and settled for one which would suit his needs. He quickly did a Google map search for Thomas's street. It took seconds and he was relieved to discover that it was less than a kilometre from the store.

He set off and walked down the streets that were lined with beautiful Jacaranda **trees.** Their purple foliage and the fallen petals cast a carpet onto the footpath and for a moment he felt himself relax a little.

The houses were mainly bungalows with perfect brickwork and elaborate **quoins that** made them look as if they had been designed to bring a sense of solidarity and harmony. Their gardens were full of trees, roses and shrubs, each neatly tended but without the look of monotonous regularity. It was he thought a suburb that reflected what every street should look like. Why was it only those who lived in the affluent suburbs who were able to enjoy street trees? Why weren't there trees like this throughout all of the suburbs including the poor ones where streets lay bare and harsh and ugly houses sat sulking in their poverty whilst their occupants lived lives of struggle and occasionally despair.

He shook of his moment of despondency and focussed on the beauty around him. He could hear the birds in the trees and from the distance came the raucous call of a kookaburra. He was so absorbed in his surroundings he was surprised to see that he was two houses away from where Thomas lived. He felt his nervousness come back a he tried to prepare himself in explaining what was happening to Thomas. How would Thomas respond?

He slowed down and stopped out of the front of Thomas's house. It was similar to the others and had a giant Golden ash tree in the middle of the lawn and the perimeter of the garden was surrounded by roses. They were in all shades of pink and he could smell the perfume as he stood by the wrought iron gate that was embellished with swirls of cleverly crafted iron mongering.

As he stood there a woman came out. She was wearing gardening gloves and had a pair of secateurs in her hand. She looked tired and her hair was untidy. She had a strained look on her face which her large garden hat couldn't disguise.

He had not been prepared to see anyone but Thomas. Now he had no idea what to say.

She looked at him and came towards him and as she did she took off her hat that was obscuring her vision. 'My God. You're exactly like my son Thomas. It's incredible.' She stood staring at him and he began to feel embarrassed by her scrutiny. Finally she looked away and when she looked back at him he saw her looking puzzled.

'I've seen you before haven't I? But I can't quite . . .' she broke off her conversation then snapped her fingers. 'You were in the hospital. I saw you there and thought how much you looked like Thomas. I wasn't very close but I had no idea that you'd look like his identical twin. It's incredible.'

'I've never met him so I wouldn't know how much alike we are. My name's Zerach. I was going for a walk and I stopped to have a look at your roses. I love the smell of them.'

'It's a passion of mine,' she said but there was no excitement in her voice which was flat and depressed. He could see that she was making an effort even to speak to him but in spite of her feeling she smiled at him. 'I'm Thomas's mum as you've probably guessed. 'I'm a physiatrist at the hospital which is where I saw you. The roses help me cope or at least they used to but things have been . . .' He saw that she was close to crying but she brushed aside her tears and took off her hat. 'I must look a mess with my daggy clothes and silly old garden hat. But before you go you must meet my son. I can't imagine what his reaction is going to be. Come in.'

She took off her gloves and left them on a wicker chair on the veranda. She opened the door and they went down a long passage whose old wooden floors gleamed and he saw large paintings that seem to cover every space that was available.

'Thomas should be **in** the kitchen. We were going to have some lunch. You must join us.' **He saw the effort it took her even to speak and the skylight** showed up her features more clearly he saw that she was more than tired, she was exhausted. There were large bags under her eyes which were red and sore and long lines of sorrow ran down her face.

He felt that he had intruded on some private grief. Perhaps, he thought he should make up an excuse and come back hopefully when she was a work. He was about to offer his apologies when she ushered him into the large kitchen. It had a huge, old oak table in the middle of the room and over it hung a picture of a mountain. Hovering over the mountain were three spheres. **It was both beautiful and ethereal and he longed to touch them but knew that wasn't possible. How could it be that his three spheres were in the house? He knew that it couldn't be a coincidence and he had to force himself not to blurt out everything that he knew about them.**

He saw Thomas sitting with his back to him. Thomas half turned to see who his mother had brought with her and he froze. After a moment he stood up but he was, it seemed unable to speak. They looked at each other and said nothing. Words couldn't convey what they felt. They were mirror images of each other. Crafted and made exactly the same. Eyes, mouth, hair, and the shape of their chins.

'Well for heaven's sake. One of you has to speak.' She waited but still, they kept looking at each other and at last Zerach held out his hand. Thomas shook it and he felt as if he was connected to something that had been missing from him since his birth.

'Grab a seat,' said Thomas.

'Hop in,' Thomas said. 'It's only bread and cheese and some old olives but help yourself.

Zerach didn't feel very hungry after his quick meal at the shopping centre but he took some bread and cheese and waited for the others to start eating. It was obvious, however, that neither of them was hungry. **They both tore off tiny bits of the bread and nibbed at an olive and bits of cheese.** Thomas looked at Zerach and Zerach knew that Thomas was aware of the mood they were conveying. 'Mum I'm sorry,' Thomas said 'I'm not hungry.'

'You have to eat something Thomas. It's been days and neither of us has eaten a thing.'

'I know Mum. I'll take some outside and then I and Zerach can get to know each other better. It's not every day you meet your twin.' Hannah nodded and they left. They went out to the back veranda and

Thomas flopped down on a chair. 'Sit down Zerach. I'm not really sure what to say to an undiscovered look alike.'

Zerach wished he could find some way into a conversation that was going to sound unbelievable. There was, he realised, no gentle way so he cleared his throat and began. 'I need to tell you about something that is going to sound bizarre and you'll probably think I'm crazy. Can I ask you to listen to me and not interrupt until I've finished.'

'So why not just start at the beginning and finish at the end? That's what my English teacher is always on about when we have to write dopey stories. So I'm ready. Shoot.'

Zerach told him everything that had happened. He started with his dreams and told Thomas about the spheres and about Reuben.

'And you said the spheres you saw in our picture are the same as the ones that you saw in your dreams? That's cool.'

'Is it?' Zerach said. 'I thought that you'd think I was crazy.'

'Well I have to wait until you finish your story then I'll tell you. So keep going. If I get up and run away it means that you've lost me.' Thomas laughed and Zerach relaxed and plunged in. 'This is going to sound weird but here goes. I'm supposed to find four people. I've found you. You're my twin and that's obvious at least as far as we look like each other. Then I'm supposed to find two others who like us . . . like us. . .' He couldn't say it. Saying that they all had been chosen and had a mission to stop the darkness was too much like a science fiction story to be credible. Thomas, however, simply waited then said: 'Go on you can't stop now. You're too far in to retreat.'

'Okay. No more chickening out. There are four of us. Each of us is special. Very special. In fact unique. They have been waiting for hundreds of years for us and now it's time. We have to find the other two and stop the darkness from getting worse.'

'What darkness?' Thomas said. Zerach looked at Thomas closely. 'I think you've seen it or felt it haven't you? Tell me I'm not crazy.'

'You're not. I felt it. In the mine. And in the attic. It was something strange and scary so that's why when you started to tell me everything I had a feeling that you were here for something special.'

Thomas told him about his father and the fact that he'd gone missing in the blackness of the mine. He told him also of the strange bird in the attic and how it had attacked him and how he had felt its hatred and malevolence as if it were a real person and not just a bird. When Zerach had mentioned Reuben Thomas excitedly told him about Sophia and how Sophia and Reuben seemed similar.

'So something is actually happening?' asked Thomas.

'Yes and we don't have a lot of time. I know it's going to get a lot worse.'

'And how do we find the other two? Come to that, how did you find me?'

'I saw your photo on the posters you put up. I also saw your house on the news when they reported about your dad. It was easy to Google your street. Nothing special about what I did.'

'You found me. That's special. When I first saw you it was as if I had been waiting for you for all of my life. Like there was a part of me that was missing and now it isn't. **So** how do we stop the darkness and what is it that it's trying to do? I know it can make you feel like crap and you get depressed but there are millions of people who have depression. It's a medical condition. You're not trying to tell me that everyone who has depression is a victim of this thing are you?' Thomas asked.

'No. Not at all. It can use depression when it's targeting people like us. People who represent a threat to it. It did it to both of us. It takes away all hope. But I think there's a lot more that's going to happen.'

'So what is going to happen?' Thomas asked.

Zerach had been Dreading this question even though he knew that sooner or later it was a question that would be asked. He tried to think of something to say but as the silence grew between them he started to wonder if he'd said too much too soon. He knew however, he had to go on. He had no choice.

'I don't really know but I feel as if something terrible is about to happen. Reuben said that they've waited for centuries for the four of us to come together. The spheres keep talking to me and each time they get more intense. I'm scared and feel totally out of my depth. How can four of us fight this thing? **It's something** that we don't really know and don't understand?'

'We just find the others and get things moving.' Thomas said nonchalantly. 'If what you say is true we can't be sitting around on our bums. We have to find them. When do we start?'

'Now, but I don't know how.'

'Oh,' Thomas said obviously disappointed.

'I'm sorry. I'm supposed to be the one who knows what to do but I don't have a clue.'

'Crap Zerach. You've had heaps of clues and with my dad missing I know something bad is happening. You know what you have to do it's just that you haven't done it before.'

'What do I do then Thomas? Wave that stick in the air and something magical will happen like in Harry Potter?'

'No dick head. Think.'

'I can't think of anything! I told you already.'

'Yes you did. But what's something that you've never tried before?'

'Apart from finding you I haven't done anything.'

'Who gave you the dreams?' Thomas asked patiently as **if it was him** and not Zerach who knew more about what to do than Zerach himself.

'The spheres. I've told you that already.'

'Yes you did. So what do you do next when you need their help?'

'Ask them?' Zerach said trying to keep the terror out of his voice. 'Are you sure?'

'You know the answer to that already.'

Zerach nodded but he felt like a schoolboy who had been asked to perform in front of a school assembly on an instrument he had never seen before, let alone played.

CHAPTER TWENTY SEVEN

'I need time to think,' Zerach said **knowing that he** was simply stalling for time.

'Fair enough. Come back tomorrow. Go home. Sleep and I'll see you first thing in the morning.'

'There's a small problem.'

'What?'

'I can't go home.'

'Why not?'

'Because I escaped from the psych ward of the hospital and if I go home mum and dad will take me back. They think I'm schizophrenic.'

'Shit Zerach. They'll be out looking for you.'

'Mum and dad will be frantic. I never even stopped to think to give them a call and let them know I'm okay.'

'That's easily fixed. Ring them and I'll ask mum if you can stay with us. My mum will say yes especially as dad's still missing so you'll take her mind off him for a while. It'll be neat.'

'You make everything sound so easy.'

'Well this bit is easy enough. I'm a bit spooked out about the spheres though.'

'But you just said . . .'

'I know what I said but you're the hero not me.'

'Some hero I am.'

'That's what all the heroes say. You'll surprise yourself and me too since I'll be right next to you when you ask for their help.'

'Thanks Thomas for letting me stay. I thought I'd be sleeping on a park bench or in a cardboard box.'

'I think it might be a bit more comfortable here than a cardboard box but not much. The couch is crap to sleep on but you'll be fine. Besides, you'll be too busy to sleep because you'll be working out how to contact the spheres.'

'Thanks Thomas. Are you sure your mum will be okay with me staying?'

'Yep. She likes having my friends over and because you're here she'll make a proper meal tonight. I miss dad and I'm worried but I'm starting to get sick of having baked beans on toast for tea.'

'But I could see that you were both finding it hard even to eat a bit of bread and cheese at lunch.'

'I think she felt guilty about the rubbishy food we've been eating. So with a bit of luck you'll have a nice meal as well as the **world's** worst couch. Can't make a better offer than that eh?' Thomas smiled and Zerach knew that Thomas was using banter to cover up his pain. He wished he knew the right words to say but knew that words, even skilful ones wouldn't change anything.

They went inside and heard Thomas's mother moving about in the front garden. 'It's her way of coping or at least trying to. It's really horrible thinking about dad all of the time. I know that she's starting to think that he might have fallen down a shaft and . . .'

'You don't have to say it Thomas.'

'I do. I don't want to but it's what I think. I don't think he could survive for long in the mine. If he fell down he may have been killed or if not he would have died from his injuries. I know this will sound wrong but if he did die I hope it was quick. It would be unbearable lying in the dark and being injured and no-one being able find you. I'd go mad. Come on. Thinking about dad just makes it worse. Let's drag mum away from the garden. I'll help with the cooking. Normally she won't let me anywhere near her when she's preparing a meal but I think she'll be pleased that I'm there with her.'

After their meal they all watched a movie but Zerach could see that Thomas's mother was miles away, locked in her pain from which there seemed to be no escape. When the movie was finished she left the room and as if suddenly realising that she hadn't said anything she bade them good night.

Thomas looked at his mobile phone. 'It's after twelve. Time you turned in. You never know, perhaps the spheres will come to you in a Dream like they have before.' For some reason Zerach knew that wasn't going to happen and too soon he was lying on the couch going over all that had happened that day. His parents had begged him to come home when he'd called them shortly after he and Thomas had come inside but he assured them he was fine. In the end he had to hang up. His mother had been crying and his father was frantic.

'Please come home, son. We can talk things over. If you really don't want to go back to hospital then maybe we can convince Dr Michal to let you stay home for a few days. I'll take time off work and we can spend time together like we used to when you were little.'

Zerach had listened to his father and he knew that his father was trying not to sound like he was pleading but Zerach knew that he was. He also knew that his parents would call Dr Michal and that would be it. He'd be back in hospital with no hope of escape. Dr Michal would make sure of that.

He hung up as his dad was half way through a sentence. He couldn't cope with their fear and pleading. He felt as if he was abandoning them but he knew he couldn't bear to listen for another minute. He felt exhausted and needed to rest. The couch was as uncomfortable as it looked. It had four cushions but they each seemed to sag at different places and he barley slept.

At last the morning light shone through the curtains. Seven o'clock. He got up from the couch and wondered what to do. He had no idea what time Thomas or Hannah would be up so he walked outside and sat on the back veranda looking over the small hill that was just visible through the trees.

He shivered. He knew that he was looking at the tin mine and he tried to get the image out of his mind of Thomas's father being trapped in the dark or worse lying there dead. How, he wondered, could they even get out of bed at all? How was it that Hannah could go to the market and buy cheese, make bread and try at least to have a simple lunch?

They were, he realised, stronger than he was. Either that or they were putting on a front for his benefit but as soon as he thought that he knew it wasn't true. He knew that it was far too soon for them to be getting on with their lives. They were supporting each other and trying to maintain some remnant of normality. It was this that was keeping them from the horrors that he knew must torment them, each night not sleeping properly and hoping and perhaps praying that some sort of miracle would occur.

The longer he thought about them the more agitated he became. Finally he was unable to sit still any longer. He set off. He had no idea where he was going but he followed a rough track and heard the birds in the massive Blue Gums that were sporadically dotted through the property.

He came to a fence and climbed over it and continued walking. He had stopped taking notice of where he was going. He simply followed his feet as if they knew where to go even if he didn't.

He approached a hill and after walking for some time he saw the signs of the old mines. He struggled to find the entrance but after searching on his hands and knees he finally found it. He shuddered. It was dark and cold and gave off an air of misery and despair. This, he knew, was what Thomas had felt. He knew too that this was some small part of the darkness. It's presence he knew was not safely contained in the mine. It was beyond time and he now realised beyond space. It could go where it pleased. In an attic. In a mine. And it could ooze into one's mind and bleed its blackness into **one's** psyche.

He had to get back. The feeling of oppression was growing stronger and he felt it begin to pull him further into the cave. He resisted but to his horror he felt himself going into the entrance and before he knew it he was crawling along the main shaft heading into a darkness that he had not imagined was possible.

The harder he tried to stop the stronger its pull seemed to get. He was in too deep. Had he taken a different tunnel? Was he lost? Would, he too, be like Thomas's father and disappear into the gloom and no-one would have any idea where he had gone? He started to sob as he felt it Drawing him in, ever closer- a fish trapped on a hook. He could now feel its emotions. It was exalting in his misery. It relished his pain and suffering and he knew that soon, he too, would be gone.

He was seconds away from succumbing. He closed his eyes. He knew he was done. He waited and decided that if he was going to die he would somehow find the courage to do so with his eyes open.

He saw something. It was a dim glow or was it his last feeble attempt at survival? He looked again. Was if a fraction less dark than before? His eyes began to water from the stain of trying to see something that was barley there.

The light started to get brighter. He held his hand in front of his face. He could see his hand. The light continued to grow brighter. He could now see the roughly hewn edges of the rock that had been gouged out when the mine was being dug. He saw colours. They shimmered and came towards him. They hovered over his head. He saw the three of them. It was his spheres. Thomas was right. Only he had not found them. They had found him.

They danced around him shimmering about him in with their effervescent glow. He felt their joy. Their love. He felt the darkness move. It was withdrawing but Zerach knew that it was not beaten. It would wait and he saw into its mind. It was delighting in its plan. Soon, it thought, the world would tremble and then it would destroy the planet that these creatures called the earth.

CHAPTER TWENTY EIGHT

Zerach pulled his mind back from the creature of darkness. Led by the spheres he followed their light and to his joy he saw daylight. He crawled out and turned to see where the spheres were. They had gone. He felt disappointed at their departure but his main feeling was one of gratitude.

He'd not known what to do but when he needed them they'd appeared. He needed to tell Thomas what had happened. Now feeling buoyant he started to jog taking care to follow the same path as before.

He looked at his mobile to check the time. Four fifty it said. He stopped. It must be wrong. He knew that he'd not been that long in the mine. How could it be four fifty? Feeling confused he jogged a little faster. He'd gone for about three hundred metres when he heard Thomas calling out his name.

Thomas was at the branch in the path that led back to the house. 'Where have you been Zerach? Mum and I have been looking for you all day. What do you think you're doing just pissing off like that? Shit Zerach, mum has enough to worry about without her thinking that you've disappeared. Why didn't you tell us what you were doing? I thought I could trust you but no you just rack off on your own saying bugger all.'

Zerach was shocked by the anger in Thomas's voice. How could he explain the amoung of time that he'd been away? He tried to think of what best to say but before he could speak Thomas rushed up to him and stood glaring at Zerach.

'We started looking for you first thing this morning and guess what? You'd decided to go off exploring for nearly eight hours. Eight! Can you imagine what it's been like?'

'Thomas please let me explain.'

'Why should I let you explain anything? Why don't you just bugger off back to the loony bin where you belong?'

The darkness gloated. It had manufactured a fracture between the twins. 'Loony bin' was the phrase it needed Thomas to say delighting Zerach's pain.

'Loony bin? Loony bin? No-one says that anymore. I told you. I'm not sick!'

'Oh yes. And what little adventure did you have while you were away chasing fairies or gnomes or whatever else you were up to?'

Zerach could see that Thomas was shocked. This wasn't the Thomas he knew. He wanted to reach out. To touch him and bring him back. But how?'

'Can you please, please give me ten minutes to talk to you?'

'That's ten minutes too long.'

'Thomas you have every right to be angry but can you see that you're saying things that you wouldn't normally say? It's that thing. It's got to you somehow.'

'What thing would that be?'

'I called it The Darkness. I don't know what it is but it's far, far stronger than either of us understands.'

'I understand only too well. You're full of . . .'

'Listen to me! Please! You're not being yourself.'

'So I've morphed into a creature from the abyss?'

'No. The creature from the abyss has you by the throat only you don't know it.' Zerach needed the spheres. He needed Thomas to see them. But how?

He looked at the beauty around him and heard the joy of the bush and the swishing of the branches as they played in the wind. He saw the blue of the sky and the pied beauty of a magpie as it landed on a branch over their heads. This was the world of the spheres. They encapsulated all that was beauteous and good. He knew that Thomas needed to see them for him to believe but didn't know how to do it or if it was even possible.

As if Thomas had read his mind he abruptly said 'If you show me the spheres then I'll believe you. If you can't, just go.'

'But . . .'

'No excuses. No buts. **No saying later, just show me.**'

'I'm not sure I can.' Zerach looked imploringly at Thomas but his face was red with anger. No, Zerach thought. It was more than anger. **It** was hatred.

His twin looked so different. Gone were his kind features and his sense of friendliness and openness. He was a different person. The transformation was shocking to see. Even Thomas's eyes were different. Where was the kindness and humanity that used to shine from them? They were cold, callous and malicious.

Zerach tried to think of what to do. Could he summon the spheres? No. That was not how they worked. They would not be summoned but they might be asked or even prayed for. He did not believe in prayer but he had to try.

He knew he would need all of his powers of concentration and his power, if it really existed. He recalled their beauty and their power and the love and mystery that they contained. He saw in his mind's eye how they looked in the mine and how they danced and dazzled him with their beauty. He longed for them. He needed them to Drive out what had happened to Thomas.

He lifted his head and felt the sun on his face and how it shone through his closed eyes. He kept on looking at the faint red that he could see and for the first time he had left the synagogue he prayed.

He didn't know how long he stood with his face to the sun but after what seemed an age he heard the squawking of parrots as they flew overhead. The noise grew louder and Thomas looked up and saw dozens of parrots land in the tree above them.

The noise of the parrots grew. More and more birds arrived. Thousands of them now filled the tree and festooned it in colour.

Blue, green, red and yellow. A kaleidoscope of colour that made the tree blossom with life.

Thomas looked up and then looked at Zerach. He was distracted but the birds in the tree were not enough to convince him. He took a step closer to Zerach and as he did the birds took flight.

They circled over their head three times. Now there were thousands- a vast number of birds had congregated together and were flying around them. They flew closer and closer to their heads and then they did something extraordinary. They split into three massive flocks and fluttered over them in a pattern that formed three circles.

They shimmered with colour and then three of the birds landed and sat next to his feet. They sat there if they were tame and not creatures of the wild. They fluttered their wings and then joined the others in their circular dance over Zerach and Thomas.

Behind them a rainbow appeared. It shone in the sky and the birds flew towards it and then were gone. The three birds next to Zerach, however, did not leave. They sat there as if he was a companion **as if it were a being** with whom they wished to stay. Thomas looked at Zerach. He had changed. He had not seen the spheres but he had witnessed something extraordinary and inexplicable. It was enough.

'I don't know what to say. I've never seen anything like that happen before. It's hard to believe but I saw it with my own eyes. 'You are special Zerach. I'm sorry I was saying those terrible things about you. Part of me knew what was happening but I couldn't control it.'

'It's okay. I could tell that something or more accurately that something had taken control of you. You looked so different.'

'I could feel it in me Zerach. I tried to stop it but I couldn't.'

'Well you're back that's the main thing.' Zerach said. Thomas looked at the birds and laughed. 'Looks like you've got some new friends.'

'I think they're more than that. I'm not sure what's happening and it's definitely not by chance. Somehow I think that we need them and I think we both know who sent them.'

'It was the spheres wasn't it?'

'Yes, but I don't know why they didn't come themselves.'

'Perhaps you're the only one who's allowed to see them?'

Zerach didn't want to agree with Thomas. It would, he thought, sound arrogant but he thought that Thomas was right. They arrived back at the house and went into the kitchen. Hannah was sitting at the table looking at the painting of the spheres. She turned and rushed towards Zerach. 'Thank God you're okay. I thought that something terrible had happened. I even thought that you'd gone into the mine but in the end I thought that you may have left. I can't pretend that I didn't feel hurt and confused but now here you are. At the end of the day it's all that matters'

'I'm sorry Dr Weinstock. I went for a walk and got lost. Luckily for me Thomas managed to find me.'

'Well as long as you're safe. You must be hungry. I'll make something to eat.' She started to prepare the meal and Thomas indicated that they should go into the lounge room.

'She looks terrible. Obviously there's still no news about dad. I wish I could help her but how can I? We're both grieving but it's horrible not knowing what happened.'

'I don't know what to say other than I'm sorry.'

'If only sorry would bring him back eh?' Thomas asked. 'But the world doesn't work like that does it?'

Zerach was tempted to say something platitudinous but stopped himself. The last thing that Thomas needed to hear was something facile. Besides, Thomas looked exhausted so he said nothing. After a few moments Zerach looked out of the window. The three birds were perched on the rail of the veranda.

'They're still with us,' said Thomas as he went to the window and stood beside Zerach. I wonder what they're here for? ' Thomas's question took Zerach by surprise. He was about to mumble some vague answer when something deep inside of him rushed to the surface. 'They're here to show us how to find the others. We need to get the four of us together as soon as we can. We need to follow the birds. They're our guides sent by the spheres.'

Zerach could see that Thomas was excited to be involved in something that was so mysterious. 'We start tomorrow,' said Zerach.

He was surprised to hear the certainly in his voice. He knew that he had gained strength from the spheres and the birds that they had been sent to help them. All they needed to do was to see where the birds would lead them. He hoped it would prove to be as simple as it sounded.

CHAPTER TWENTY NINE

The morning light shone onto Thomas's curtains. He went down to the kitchen and found Zerach packing his bag. A half eaten banana sat on the table and a bowl of cereal had congealed with the milk forming a thick sludge.

'Nice breakfast.'

'Couldn't eat even though I know we must. We need to be ready when the birds show us the way to the other two.'

'But how can you be so sure that they will? I know what happened yesterday but this morning I'm not so sure.'

'You can't allow yourself to have any doubts. I can ride my bike to the cycle shop. I can dinky you there and we'll buy you a bike.'

'I haven't got any money.'

'I have a card. Don't ask how but it's all taken care of. If we need something we can buy it. You'll just have to trust me.

'So we leave today?'

'I think so Thomas. We'll see what the birds are up to in a minute.'

Thomas went to the kitchen cupboard and pulled out a note pad and started to scribble a note to his mum. He was halfway though it when he put down the pen. 'I'm sorry Zerach but I can't come. I can't leave mum here by herself. It's not right. She's barely coping and I'm leaving her. I know that something terrible is happening but why me? There are thousands of teenagers in South Australia and my dad's missing and mum's grieving and I simply leave her? I can't do it. You're asking too much of me.'

'Thomas I'm not asking you to do anything. The spheres are and something more than that which I don't really understand. You are one of the four who've been chosen. There has to be a reason for that. You can't back out now. You've felt this creature in the attic. It's real and it scares me too. I'm leaving my parents and they don't even know where I am. They think I'm unwell and need to be in hospital. I had no say over being chosen either. I can't change the fact that we're needed. That you're needed. There's something terrible about to happen and only we four can change it or at least try to. You have to come Thomas. Please this is too important.'

He saw the struggle that Thomas was going through. His mother needed him. That was a fact. His father was missing and could be dead and he was being asked to leave. At least Zerach knew that his parents were alive. How, he wondered would he respond if he were in Thomas's shoes? Would he too refuse the call? He didn't know but he longed to comfort Thomas, to tell him that everything was going to be okay and yet he didn't know what was going to happen so he knew that he could not lie to him.

'I can't force you to come. It's a choice that you have to make. I hope that you'll come but it's your decision.'

'I don't want to decide. I want things to go back to normal. I want dad back and mum to be happy, but that's not going to happen is it?'

'I have a friend. **He's name is Reuben check if Thomas knows.** He helped me and I think that if I ask him he'll help your mother. If I can get him to come do you think that you may change your mind?'

'Can you do that?'

'I hope so Thomas. For all of our sakes I hope that I can because if I can't, then I have no idea what the creature is really capable of doing. Let me try.' He closed his eyes and imagined Reuben standing in the kitchen talking to Hannah. He envisioned Reuben's wisdom and begged him to come. He urged the spheres to intervene on his behalf and he prayed, to whom he didn't know, but he imagined a power that was beyond everything that he knew or would ever be capable of knowing. Of goodness so pure that it was perfection personified. It was a being that had created the world and had wrought from a formless void, a planet as beautiful as earth.

He felt the air shimmer and he felt an electric charge run through his body. He felt Reuben's presence and experienced the creators love flow through him. He felt its endless peace and total acceptance of him and of all creatures. It was a love so boundless that if filled him with gratitude so profound that he wept at the beauty of it.

He heard his name being called. He recognised the voice. It came from the front door. He rushed to it and flung the door open and threw himself into Reuben's arms. Reuben held him as if he was the most precious thing in the world. He hugged him and Zerach felt his compassion which, he now knew, came from a source higher than them all.

'Thought I'd pay you a visit,' Reuben said, 'and of course to meet your twin and Hannah. He walked in and plonked himself at the table as if he were a regular guest and smiled at Thomas who was standing by the table looking at Reuben in disbelief. 'You're Rueben aren't you? I don't know how I can possibly know that but I do.'

'You know that Thomas because you have been called. Like Zerach **you** have a precious gift that needs to be treasured and honoured. I know how you feel about leaving your mother behind but you must. It's a terrible thing to ask of you but yet I am here to ask you to reconsider. You've seen what the spheres can do and you witnessed the miracle of the birds. You know that this isn't a natural thing. It transcends the natural. Can you see that dear child?'

'I know. I know. But why me?'

'I have known many extraordinary people who have asked exactly the same question. Some heeded the call. Some did not. Those who did defied what was considered to be normal or even the right thing to do, yet they **still** went. Without these people your world and its people would not have progressed. You and humans are capable of great deeds and also great horrors. Sometimes one must act even as they quiver and shake in fear but yet go out and follow the call. You are called and you will suffer. But the world will, with you, and the other three, may be able to resist the evil that is rising and growing in its strength. It is up to you to decide what it is that you will do.'

'And mum? What will become of her if I accept?'

'She will grieve as millions have before her. She will survive and with time learn to cherish the love she had for her husband. All humans suffer. It can destroy you or it can make you grow in compassion. Your mother will **in time** find peace. You too will grieve. Because of your grief you will work with those who are grief stricken and bring them comfort and hope. All this could happen in your future. The evil rises and must be faced. I wish that there was another way but there is not. Choose wisely Master Thomas.'

Thomas looked at Reuben and looked at Zerach. He knew what he had to do. He would, he knew suffer, but not to heed the call would be to throw back a gift-a gift that with the others could stop the evil that sought to destroy creation.

'I will go with the others,' Thomas said. Reuben hugged him and went up to the painting. The spheres will give some comfort to your mother. She will remember Daniel and his love each time she looks at the picture. In time it will give her joy. Now I must go and let you get on with what you are going to do.' He got up and looked at the picture and smiled. Then he was gone.

Zerach and Reuben sat at the table not knowing what to say. They heard the clock ticking each tick reminding Zerach that time was passing too quickly. He was reluctant to get up. The aura of Rueben still clung to the room and he didn't want to leave it. To his surprise Thomas stood up and glanced at the painting. **'Time to go,' he said.**

They walked out into the bright sunshine and saw how the dew had make Droplets of water form on the branches of the trees. A magpie carolled in the distance and a small mob of kangaroos bounded across the paddock and soon disappeared amongst the scrub.

The day was perfect and it seemed to represent the antithesis of what they knew they must face. Whatever this thing was, it was they knew **its** hated **of** nature's beauty.

They heard the birds before they saw them. The noise was extraordinarily loud. **It was** far too loud to be coming just from three parrots. They looked up. The trees were covered. Their canopies loaded down with the weight of a massive flock of crows.

The birds saw them and took to the air. There were thousands of crows circling over them casting a dark shadow as they flew above them.

They swooped towards Zerach and Thomas. In a few seconds they were surrounded. They ran back to the house but the birds had anticipated their intentions. A dozen or more were between them and the safety of the house. As they ran the birds attacked. They landed on their heads and starting pecking at their scalps. Soon blood was running down both Zerach and Thomas's faces. They tried to cover their eyes but the birds landed on their arms and viciously tore at their flesh. Half blind with blood they tried to keep running but the weight of the birds was forcing them to the ground. The birds gave a craw of victory. Zerach and Thomas tried to fend them off but they knew that it was impossible to fight against so many of them.

'Do something Zerach. They'll kill us!' Zerach heard the desperation in Thomas's voice. Frantically Zerach called out for the spheres. Nothing. He called again but there were no lights or colours only the blackness of the birds and his pain.

He waited but then knew that this time they were not coming. He felt his terror rise. It had become impossible to escape as the birds hacked at their flesh. With each peck, fresh blood sprang from their wounds. By now they were covered in blood and swarms of flies landed on their flesh and started supping at this communion gift.

Thomas knew that he couldn't last. He rolled over, and although he crushed a few of the birds all he had achieved was to expose another part of himself to their frenzy. He tried to stand but they attacked his face. It was his eyes that they wanted. He would be blinded and he knew what their fate would be.

The crows exalted. They were going to destroy the twins. Zerach's world had shrunk to one of pain and terror. He had been abandoned. He and Thomas were going to die. He thought he heard Reuben's voice. It was dim and indistinct but it was him wasn't it? He tried to call to him but felt too weak. Would he come again so soon or had they used up their last chance with Reuben when he had called to him not long before.

He stopped struggling. He was beaten. They were beaten. Zerach looked at his twin but all he could see was his sneakers. The rest of him was smothered by the crows. Thomas needed Zerach and he could do nothing. Where was his power now? he mocked. Reuben's' face floated into his vision. 'Unless you find your power and use it Zerach, you will die. You must look inside of yourself and discover who you are before it's too late.'

He imagined a light, brighter than the sun, brighter than a thousand suns. He could feel their heat and their immense energy. He felt it glimmer in him. It was feeble but it was there. He looked deeper into himself. The light grew stronger. He felt its power and the light of the cosmos. Slowly he began to draw on their power. Their power was his power. He felt it beginning to course through him. He saw the massive flares of each sun as it reached out sending out vast plumes of light and heat.

The power continued to grow in him. Surely he could not contain such power? It was immense. He would have to release it or he felt it would destroy him. He lifted his arms to the sky. He felt his body shudder and he released his power. He heard the roll of thunder and flashes of lightening skewered the sky. The wind swirled around him and formed an eddy that nearly lifted him off the ground. The air itself seemed to be alive and he looked at the birds and directed his energy at them.

He felt the birds' sudden fear. He continued to hold his arms to the sky and rays of fire shone out of his body. The birds shrivelled, and then were reduced to ash. Light continued to cascade out of him. The valley was flooded with it. Trees shimmered, leaves became brazen with light, and flowers shook their glory into the valley.

He shook the ash from his body and went to Thomas. He too was covered in ash and lay still as if he were dead. 'Thomas. They've gone. I've destroyed them.'

Thomas didn't move. Zerach allowed a small part of his power to enter into Thomas. Thomas groaned and sat up. Blood flowed from him and seeped into the earth. Zerach entered into himself again. His friend could die. He would not let that happen. He imagined the blood stopping and Thomas's wounds healing.

'You're not bleeding! How can you not be bleeding? They were tearing us to pieces and you don't have a mark on you.'

'Nor do you Thomas.' Thomas looked. There were no wounds. No cuts, no bruises no blood. No pain. 'You have found your power haven't you?' Zerach nodded and embraced his twin. 'I think so.' He smiled.

The darkness withdrew. It would have to be more cautious but it too had powers that Thomas was not aware of. It needed to act quickly. It sent out part of itself into an unexplored part of the Amazon rain forest. It needed to test its strength before using it to do more – far, far more.

The green canopy was alive with monkeys, birds, insects and their sounds could be heard through the trees. The huge trees had struggled upwards to find the light leaving those who were less successful to languish in the gloom below. Ants scurried about collecting dead insects and laboriously taking them back to their nests.

The Amazon River was full of life. Fish darted about and birds hovered over the river seeking a meal. The mist rose up from the ground and hung softly over the lushness of the forest.

Out of the greenness, a black hole appeared on the damp ground. Vegetation disappeared and the small animals that had been scampering over the floor of the forest **disappeared**. The hole grew bigger. It snaked around the base of the giant trees, and, as **it** did their trunks were wrapped in darkness. It continued upwards. Inexorably the trees, animals and part of the river disappeared. Where there had been a forest, rich and vibrant with life, all had been swallowed into the void. The creature was pleased. It had started and now nothing would stop it. All would be returned to the void. The black silence would once **more reign in triumph over its domain.**

In the jungle, a small hunting party had silently been following their prey. The leader of the group raised his blowpipe. He was about to expel the poisoned dart when he saw the darkness descend. The tree on which his prey had sat was consumed. Terrified, he lowered his blowpipe and froze. The group huddled together too afraid to speak.

It had come.

They had been told from one generation to the next for over a thousand years that the great darkness would descend. The men started keening. Their world, they knew, was going into the darkness just as their ancestors had predicted.

They stepped back and watched. As they did the hole grew bigger. Too soon it threatened to engulf them. Dropping their weapons they fled. Most escaped but two had been transfixed by what they had seen. It claimed them and exalted. It would spread its void through the planet and nothing would stop it. Thousands of years of waiting were over.

CHAPTER THIRTY

Zerach and Thomas rechecked themselves for any sign of injuries. They scanned each other but it was clear that they had been healed. Thomas was in shock. Shock at what had happened when the birds had attacked them and shock at what Zerach had done. How to speak to such a person who could, it seemed, kill birds in their thousands and heal them both? He knew that sooner or later he would have to speak but his mouth was Dry and he felt a sense of awe as he looked at Zerach.

He had only ever partially believed that Zerach was special. He had from time to time believed but deep down there remained a speck of doubt. A teenager such as Zerach ought not to exist in the modern scientific world. It was the stuff of fantasy and Greek myths. Of legends shared around a thousand fires over the millennia in indigenous cultures. Yet it was real and he had been witness to it.

'I don't know what to say Zerach. I no longer know how to treat you after seeing what you did.'

'I'm still just me. Same hair, same eyes same body, same Zerach.'

'But you're not are you? You know you're not. I don't think you really thought that you could do what you've done but you have.'

'It has.'

'It?'

'The power. I'm not sure it's me or if it merely acts through me. I'm a conduit that's all.'

'No Zerach. You're more than a conduit. That implies a passivity and lack of awareness. You're neither of those things. I saw what was coming out of your body. It was light. Pure light like I've never seen before. Your whole body was like a beacon. No. Not like a beacon. It was stronger than that. It was if . . . as if you were the sun and your body sent out its coronas into the world and destroyed a tool of something evil.

I don't know as much as you but I sense things as well. I know evil and if ever there was evil incarnate those birds were. But you know more than me. You know that something is controlling those birds and killing my dad and all that other mad stuff that's happened. That's who we have to destroy isn't it?'

Zerach wanted to deny it but he knew that Thomas had a right to know. He was part of the whole that the four of them would make. 'When the birds were attacking us I saw Reuben. He showed me how to draw on my power. He told me once, that he would only come to me three times and that was the third time. I won't see him again and I'll miss him. I wish that I could see him again but I can't. Now it seems even harder than before.

'I keep hoping that he'll come back but I know he won't.' He stopped and looked around blankly like a lost child. He made himself stop wishing for what was not going to happen. He would love and treasure Reuben but knew that he would be forever in his past. He forced himself **to** think of what needed to be done. He could not allow himself to grieve. He needed to act.

'Come on. We have to find the others and the three parrots.' Thomas nodded and they set off. As they walked away from the house they saw that the ground was littered with feathers. The ground was alive with colour but cruelly it was the colour of death. Thousands of the parrots they had seen earlier had been killed. They lay there like confetti, still beautiful even in death.

'They did this didn't they?' Thomas asked. Zerach said nothing but he knew that it was the crows that had killed them, and if so, were the bodies of the three special parrots lying dead amongst the carnage?

'It's so horrible. So cruel and sadistic.' Zerach carefully walked about the rough perimeter of where the birds lay. So many deaths. So much beauty destroyed as if they were toys to be played with then discarded.

As they stood amongst the countless feathers and breeze sprang up and the feather lifted into the air as if they were alive. It was a cruel illusion. It was unbearably beautiful and both of them felt a deep sense of anguish as they saw the feathers gradually float though the trees until all that was left was the dead birds.

'Do you think our three birds survived?' Thomas asked as he scanned the tree tops.

'I don't know. It seems unlikely. There were so many killed and that was why they were a prime target for the crows to attack. Without them we may not be able to find the others which is why it did what it did.'

'So we're stuffed?'

'No we're not. We need to find another way.'

'But how?'

'I don't know Thomas! I'm confused as well. You can't expect me to know everything.'

'No you're right. I'm sorry.'

'We need to go. I don't know. We'll follow our instincts and see what happens.'

They set off and they walked in silence for an hour each of them trying to decide what to do. Zerach had no idea where he was going. How could he possibly know where the other two were? It was impossible.

They came to a main highway and waited on the side of the road. 'We can hitchhike into Adelaide and . . .'

'I thought we were going to get me a bike,' said Thomas.

'I don't think we have enough time now that the birds have gone it's quicker to hitchhike.'

'But we don't know where we're going! How do we catch a ride to find the other two when we don't have a clue where they are? I know you said we could follow our instincts but mine aren't working. How do we find them?'

Zerach knew that he'd been rash. How easy it was to say to Thomas that his instincts would click into place like some sort of neat computer programme and there it would be. Names, addresses and anything that they needed to know.

'I've overestimated what I can do,' Zerach admitted. He knew that Thomas would be disappointed but he had to be honest. How could he summon up something like that? The event with the birds had been forced on him. He had found his strength through Reuben's help. Perhaps, he wondered, he needed a crisis to trigger off the reaction that had killed the crows? He had to learn how to use it along with the others when it was needed and not have to wait for some catastrophic event to awaken his powers.

'We'll take the first car that stops and go to the city and see what happens.'

The cars and trucks kept passing them by with the occasional Driver giving them the finger our tooting their horns and laughing at them. Finally, however, a battered old van Drew over and stopped 'Hope in. The van's shit but if we're lucky it should make it to Adelaide. I assume that's where you're headed?'

They looked at the man who was covered in tattoos and whose hair fell in long braids down his back. He wore an oversize pair of sunglasses and had a cigarette hanging out of his mouth and the radio was blasting out music from the Beach Boys.

'I'm a big fan of the Beach Boys. I know that'll sound dumb to a couple of kids your age but what the hell it's my car, my surf board on the roof rack and at this stage of my life so I figured I can do as I please. Believe it or not, until a few years ago, I used to be a banker. How mad was I?' He laughed and banged the wheel and forced cigarette into the overfull ashtray and turned up the music.

'Thanks for the ride,' Thomas said. 'We've been waiting for ages.'

'Yeah. It's getting harder and harder to have people to stop for you. Everyone is so shit scared these days, what with all of the crap that's going on. That's why I surf. It's just me, my board and the ocean. It's magic. It's the best feeling in the world. You should try it sometime.' After his initial burst of talking the man listened to the music banging his hand on the wheel it time with the beat of the music. Soon they were near the city and he slowed down.

'Will this do? It's a ten minute walk to the mall if that's where you heading. Good luck boys.' He leant over and pulled open the door. It gets stuck. Just like me in my old job but not any more eh?' He laughed again and Drove off.

They walked to the mall and quickly grabbed something to eat and Drink. They stood next to **the** silver orb that was the main sculpture in the mall and watched as the throngs of people hurried past them. 'I don't think this is where we're supposed to be,' Zerach said. 'Do you have any ideas?' Thomas looked surprised but without hesitation he knew where they should go. He felt a flush of pride that he did have some inner knowledge that at this moment that Zerach didn't.

'We need to go the fountain outside of the museum. Don't ask me how I know because I can't give you an answer.'

'See you can know things. At the moment I feel lost but you knew what to do.' Zerach saw that Thomas was trying to hide his discovery of what he knew and Zerach didn't. He watched him as his face changed and he squared his shoulders then led the way.

The fountain splashed its water onto the pavers that surrounded it and parents sat with their children feeding the pigeons that were strutted about self importantly. Zerach and Thomas sat down of the edge of the fountain and a white dove landed near them. A few moments later another two landed. They stood apart from the other birds and seemed to be waiting.

'I don't suppose . . . I mean . . . is it remotely possible that they're here for us or am I imagining things?' Thomas looked at Zerach waiting for his answer. As if on cue, the birds moved even closer and were now within touching distance.

'I don't know what to think. Nothing makes sense any more. So who knows? They are acting strangely for wild birds and the fact that there are three of them and they're all white doves has to mean something doesn't it?'

Thomas put his hand towards the doves and the largest of the three fluttered its wings noisily and landed on his hand. The other two followed and Thomas sat with the three white doves on him. He beamed with pleasure as he felt their trust as they walked up and down on his arms as if they had been doing this with Thomas for years. 'I think that answers your question. That thing, whatever it was, killed the three birds we needed. Now because of you it would seem that we have three doves to show us the way.'

As he finished his sentence the doves took flight and flapped above them exactly the same way as the parrots had. Thomas was right. All they had to do was follow the birds and they would be led to the others.

'There is one problem,' said Zerach.

'I know. How do we keep up with them? If we walk we'll never get there. What about the bikes.'

'We could buy them. Reuben gave me a card. He said I could use it whenever it was really needed. And we need them. There's a bike shop not far from here. We can get them and come back to the fountain.'

'But what if the birds aren't here then? What'll we do?'

'If they are what we both think they are they'll be here when we get back. It was you who led us to them and you were right. We have to trust them.'

'What I don't understand is who is doing this for us. Who can arrange for wild birds to appear and **lead** us to where we have to go. I don't understand.'

'I don't think we have to understand. We go were led. It might be the spheres or something else: something more powerful even than them.'

'You **mean** God?'

'I don't believe if God anymore but whatever it is it's a force for good. It's the opposite of the thing that made the crows kill our birds. Ever since my Dreams started I've never really understood. Perhaps we not meant to. All we can do is follow whatever it is and stop the darkness from spreading. I sure that's what it's doing. We're supposed to stop it.'

'Lucky us.' Zerach looked at his friend's face and saw his puzzlement and he gave him a light punch on the arm. 'Now you're being sardonic. See you're getting smarter by the minute.' He pulled at Thomas's sleeve and making sure that the three pigeons were still there they went looking for the bikes.

It didn't take them long to buy the bikes and they were soon back at the fountain. They leant the bikes against the cement steps of the museum and went to the fountain. 'Where are our birds?' asked Thomas. They looked but there was no white amongst the flock of pigeons.

They stood there unable to know what to do. If the birds had left all they had were two new bikes, a mobile phone and a credit card none of which were going to help them in their search.

'We'll have to wait and see if they come back. We have no alternative.' Thomas went to the bikes and pulled out his Drink bottle. As he tilted his head back he saw three white specks in the sky. As he watched they flew down and landed next to the bikes.

'Zerach! Zerach! They're here!' Zerach rushed over and saw the three doves who were patiently sitting next to Thomas. 'Well bird boy, look what you've done.' The birds waited for a few seconds and took flight. 'This is it. Lets' go.' Zerach's voice was full of excitement and they both felt buoyed up by the return of the white doves.

The birds stayed ahead of them and they followed them down King William Road and then towards Port Road. After an hour of peddling they were growing tired. They'd gone much further than they thought they would have to. They were both hungry and thirsty and finally Zerach called out to Thomas.

'I need to get something to eat and Drink. I can't keep this up for much longer. I don't even know where we are.'

'We can't stop Zerach. We don't know how long the birds will stay. We can't risk it.' Zerach knew that Thomas was right. They had no idea how long the birds would guide them. He sighed and climbed back on his bike.

'Where are they?'

'Just ahead of us. I think we're nearly there,' Thomas said.

'How can you know that?'

'The same way I thought that we'd get help in Adelaide. I don't know how. I just know.'

Wearily they fought their way up a hill and then the birds stopped. They fluttered onto a ledge of an old factory and waited. A few seconds later they flew to a small house and nestled upon a fence. **This time they did not move and sat patiently as if waiting for them to understand that this was their destination.**

'This must be it. We've made it.'

'Let's hope your right. I can't peddle for anther second.'

'What do we do now?' Thomas said.

'This has to be where they live. We knock on the door and wait.' They wheeled their bikes along the small path and placed them against the railing of the veranda. They looked at each other and taking the last step of their journey they went to the door and knocked.

CHAPTER THIRTY ONE

The Four

Scarlett jumped as she heard the knock on the door. 'Tell them to away,' she said. Darcy, however, ignored her and opened the door. 'Just tell them to go,' Darcy. 'I can't deal with anyone or anything else. Let Ms. Sayed, oops I mean Meg deal with it.'

'I think you need to see them.'

'Darcy! I told you . . .' before she could finish Darcy had gestured for them to come in. 'I think you'll say hello to these two.' He gestured for Zerach and Thomas to come in and as Scarlett struggled to get out of her chair she looked up. She knew at once who they were. Ms. Sayed had said that they would come and now they had. In spite of all of what they'd seen of Ms. Sayed's abilities they were shocked. The two young men were so alike it was impossible to tell them apart. She looked at Thomas and then at Zerach. Still too surprised to speak, she stood there waiting for them to say something.

'Sorry to barge in unannounced but we . . .'

'You're the other two. Ms. Sayed said that you'd find us and you have. I have no idea what we're supposed to do now. Do you?'

'None at all,' said Zerach, 'but in case you don't know our names I'm Zerach and this is Thomas.'

'Hi, said Darcy. 'I didn't really believe this was going to happen but here you are just like she said.

'It's strange for all of us,' said Thomas. 'Believe it or not, we were led here

by three doves. Three doves! How's that eh? Straight out of a fairy tale for children yet here we are.'

'So you believe it all? All this stuff about the darkness and what it wants to do?'

'Darcy, when I first had my Dreams I thought I was crazy. I know that Scarlett has felt it and so have you. The problem is how can we fight something we can't really see?'

'But you have seen it,' Scarlett said to Zerach.

'I've felt it and seen what it can do but I haven't seen what it looks like.'

'Does that matter?' Scarlett asked.

'I don't suppose it does really,' Zerach answered. 'Perhaps we're just supposed to wait until it appears and then . . .' Zerach hesitated and stopped. He didn't know how to continue and he looked for a moment as if were lost.

'Sit down the pair of you,' said Scarlett. 'If we have to figure this out we can't have you standing around like you're waiting for a bus.' Ms.Sayed came into the room and saw their indecision. Without any preamble she faced them and spoke.

'You have the right to refuse your quest. All of you do. You must choose this freely. Reuben has told this to Zerach and Thomas and they have accepted what they must do. Remember though Darcy, if you do nothing the world won't survive.'

'I'm sorry but you'll have to find yourself another hero.' He looked at the others and saw their looks of disapproval. 'What? Don't stand there and say nothing. You look the angriest Thomas, so get it off your chest.

Thomas hesitated then with a calmness that surprised them all he spoke. 'I've seen what Zerach did. I saw what he did with the crows. He destroyed them. I saw the rays that came out of his body. He was like the sun. It was unbelievable and yet you say that you won't fight this thing. Look at what it's done and what if that's only the beginning?

Are you going to sit on your bum and wait while Scarlett gets herself killed? Is that what you want? Hand on the baton to her and just rack off as if you don't know that you've got a gift that's incredible. But no. You just give up because you've seen it on TV and saw what it can do. Whether you like it or not isn't the point. You're one of us. There's no one else. Can you live with yourself if you do nothing and see the rest of us die?'

'**Thomas** I understand what you're saying,' said Ms. Sayed gently, 'but you and the others can't force him. He must choose freely or else you all will be defeated. I'm going to do something that I'm not supposed to. I'm going to show you what **could** happen. I'll project the future onto the TV and you can watch.

I know that it sounds impossible but all of you have experienced to some extent what the creature is like. This is what will happen if you do nothing. It may still happen even if you do decide to fight against it. Nothing is certain only the prophecy which predicted that you would all come together and that you would have enormous powers. But self doubt will jeopardise your strength. I'm not supposed to show you the future but there is too much at stake. I'll face the consequences of breaking the code that we are bidden to follow. Only time will tell if I was right to choose this path.

I'll need a few minutes to gather my strength and to resist the code. Sit while I prepare myself but do not look at me. I will change and if you see me as I really am you will be blinded.' They looked at each other but one by one they closed their eyes. The room became warm and they felt the air shimmer with power. There was a hum which turned into a deep throbbing sound. The room felt as if it was in the middle of an electric storm and the throbbing grew so loud they were forced to cover their ears.

They could feel the vibrations reverberate around the room. Soon it was as if it were part of them and they were part of it. The walls seemed to shake and the windows rattled in their frames. They heard a screeching of birds – wild, fierce and atavistic and they huddled together like children.

Gradually the noise stopped and the reverberations ceased. 'You may open your eyes. I'm sorry about the noise but one never quite knows what's going to happen when I enter my true state.' She looked at them in sympathy and they could see that she had taken a risk – a risk that she wished that she didn't have to. 'This is what will happen if you decide to do nothing. I'm sorry that you have to see it.'

A film taken from a satellite showed the future earth. The forests and jungles had been obliterated. The ice caps had melted and flooded much of the land. The oceans had risen and flooded low lying countries and hundreds of thousands of people were homeless.

The planet could no longer produce enough oxygen and the cities of the world lay broken and deserted. Millions of cars rusted on the freeways and roads as they had tried to escape the inescapable.

It was a horror that was too much for them to bear. 'Please stop,' Darcy said as the others stood weeping at their world or rather what their world had once been. Darcy sat holding hands with Scarlett and Thomas was crumpled over in despair. 'Stop it! We've seen too much.' Darcy looked at Ms. Sayed trying to stop himself from dissolving into despair grief. 'This is what will happen?'

'No Darcy this is what may happen. It is its wish, to reduce the world to its own state where it existed before the creation of the universe. It longs for the void. After earth is destroyed it will continue to ravage the universe. I'm so sorry that you had to see what may happen.'

She sighed and sat back into her chair. It was clear that she was exhausted. Her face was pale and she shook with the effort it had taken to do what she had done. The three looked at Zerach. He looked at them and finally at Ms. Sayed. 'You said that we must choose freely but how can that be after seeing that? We have no choice. You have taken it away from us.'

'No I have not. I have shown you what you need to know. You were rejecting what you didn't understand. You must have the right to make a decision based on the potential reality of what will happen. Yes, it makes it harder to say no, but if you do so, it will be a decision based on the facts and not your feelings. This is beyond your personal feelings. You must choose with your souls, not your emotions.'

'I don't believe in souls,' Zerach said.

'Whether you believe in them or not is irrelevant. What is, is. You are a spark of the divine as is all of humanity but it has lost its way. You can show them a way forward but as yet that is far in the future and only if you defeat it.'

'If I choose to.'

'If your original choice was one that was made from naivety it wasn't really a choice,' Ms.Sayed said softly. 'It was rash optimism. You assume that choices are easy. But the truest choices are those that we make knowing the risks. There are many examples of men and women who have influenced world events that have had to make choices that they didn't want to yet they did. This is the position that you find yourself in now. Make your informed choice. It's a yes or no situation.'

'I need a bit more time to think about it,' Darcy said.

'But we don't have the time Darcy,' Scarlett said.

'Darcy you are a vital part of the four. You are the chosen ones, but that does not necessarily mean that you will win. She waited for a moment and looked out of the window then she turned and faced them. 'You will need to leave Adelaide. Its next target is closer to Australia. It will attack there.'

'Where? asked Darcy as he stood and looked directly at her. 'New Zealand. Probably Christchurch. You may make what you will for it choosing that particular city with that particular name. I'll leave you to make your own decisions on its significance or lack thereof. It will, however, be soon and it is there you must go.'

'How soon is how soon?' Scarlett asked.'

'Two or three days.'

'But how can we get there in three days?' Thomas asked astonished that they were somehow expected to go overseas by themselves in few days. 'I don't have a passport,' Darcy said and I bet no one else has one either.'

'Zerach has been given a card for all of your expenses. I have passports for you all in my bag. It was arranged weeks ago.'

'But that's not possible!' Thomas said incredulously. Ms. Sayed smiled and opened her hand bag which had sat unnoticed by them next to her on the carpet. She pulled out four passports and handed each of them their passports. 'How did you know?' Darcy asked.

'You forget what we are capable of doing. It is nothing more than a trick but I must say they do look rather good don't they?' For the first time she lost her sense of solemnity and she looked almost happy as they rifled through their passports as if they were an unexpected Christmas presents.

'Oh,' she added. 'I almost forgot.' She fished into her bag again and pulled out a brochure of a hotel. 'All of the bookings have been made. As Zerach would have noticed, I've changed his age to eighteen so legally he's an adult. That will overcome any potential problems in that area. It's not the most expensive hotel nor is it the cheapest but I doubt that you'll be spending much time there in any event. Now I must let you decide as Scarlett's' mother needs me. Or to be more precise she needs her sister.' She smiled at them and left the room. They looked at each other and each of them knew that they had to act. Wordlessly they walked outside and Thomas booked an Uber cab for the next day.

The six hour flight passed quickly. They had felt secure as they flew above the clouds and were surrounded by the sun and the light. Soon, however the pilot announced that they were about to land.

They quickly passed through customs and stood outside in the weak sunshine. They called a cab and twenty minutes later they arrived at their hotel. 'So what do we do now we're here?' Scarlett asked.

'We'll wait until tomorrow,' Zerach **answered**, 'and then we go looking for it. **But** more than likely it'll be looking for us.'

It was seven o'clock in the morning when they felt the first shock wave of an earthquake. They rushed outside and saw the black mist as it began to coil around over the ground: a black snake preparing to consume its prey.

CHAPTER THIRTY TWO

The Battle Begins

'It's started,' said Thomas. Like any enemy it knew the value of surprise. Its coils detected their fear. Encouraged by their lack of action it quickened its pace. People had come out into the streets to watch, and from their hotels, tourist flocked out as if this were part of a local phenomenon made for their benefit.

'Get back!'

Zerach screamed at the throng, most of whom had their phones out videoing the coil and talking excitedly amongst themselves. 'We have to save them,' Thomas said.

'No. We can't. We have to do what we're here for. We're not the fire brigade or a rescue squad. Our purpose has been clear from the start.'

'You can't leave them!' Scarlet yelled. 'What gives you the right to decide who lives and who doesn't? I thought you were special and now you're here you don't want us to do anything.'

Zerach saw that that the three of them felt the same way. They were looking at him with a mixture of anger and amazement. 'If you don't help them you're a gutless prick'

'Darcy you have to understand . . .'

'I understand only too well. You were prepared to play the role of the hero until something like this happens and then you tell us to let them die. Well, I for one won't be following your orders. I'll go and fight it because it's obvious that you don't have the balls to do it.'

Scarlett looked at Zerach with contempt and linking her arm in Darcy's she walked towards the coil, her red hair floating above her like a beacon. Arms still linked they continued to walk towards it feeling like doomed soldiers about to disappear into the mist.

'Stop!' He commanded her. Shocked she broke away from Darcy and ran back. 'What makes you think you can stop me from going with Darcy? Unlike you, he seems to have found courage whilst yours obviously has fled

Zerach felt his rage but knew that rage was what the coil wanted. He could feel it rejoicing in their disarray. Had it had hands, it would have rubbed them together in glee. Zerach felt its hatred. It's loathing of them and especially its loathing of what they had the potential to do. But their potential was unravelling. It was winning.

'I command you to stop Scarlett.' He heard his voice but it was no longer the voice of a boy. It was the voice of a being who needed to stop this girl from destruction. Scarlett smirked and ignored him.

She tried to move her feet but they wouldn't obey her. They stayed still as if stuck on the road in cement. Zerach watched her as she leant forward trying to use the momentum of her body to make her legs move. She looked over her shoulder at Zerach. He saw rage, fear and astonishment but in spite of her turmoil she could not move.

'How did you . . .?' Thomas asked suddenly awed by what Zerach had done. Zerach ignored him. Darcy had continued to walk towards the coil that now was slithering along the ground even more rapidly. Soon it would consume its first victim and the four would be three, and three was not enough, and never would be.

Zerach was about to force Darcy to stop when he saw the coils embrace Darcy's ankles. It was an obscene embrace. Long and languishing as if it were a lover, who, having waited so long for its beloved, didn't wish to rush its embrace. Undaunted, Darcy continued to walk ahead. Too late he saw the coils gently climbing up his legs like a python ready to choke the breath out of its victim before it was eaten.

'Zerach! Thomas yelled. You stopped Scarlett, now you have to save Darcy.'

'Firstly I must bring Scarlett back to us.' He shut his eyes and focussed his mind. It took less time than he thought and Scarlett was unexpectedly free. The creature was focussing on Darcy and had give up Scarlett to maximise its chances with the boy. Again Scarlett tried to run to Darcy but Zerach forced her back to the group.

'Are you mad? You can stop me but you're letting it kill Darcy! Do something!'

'I can't do this by myself. We must work together. We don't have long so listen to what I say. Don't ask questions but follow exactly what I tell you to do. Understood? Close your eyes and in your mind create countless pictures of what it is that life offers us. Think of the things you love. Things that bring you joy and happiness. It doesn't matter what it is but it must come from your heart and more importantly form your souls. Look at what you love. Feel it. Embrace it and send those feelings and images out and direct them at the creature.

Scarlett saw Darcy. His smile, his face, his walk and his voice. She felt the love that she had for him and thought also of her troubled mother and two brothers. They had always been so difficult but she saw that each of them was unhappy and struggling to cope. She saw their pain and sent out her compassion to them. She saw their dog that was so alive and full of energy. He was called Spark and he always made her laugh. She had often looked into his eyes and had been convinced that he knew how she felt about him and he about her. She envisioned her little garden. Saw its colours as they danced in the sun bright with joy under the blue sky and of the daisy whose cheery flowers were always smiling.

Thomas though of Zerach. His twin whom he loved. Not because he was his twin but he saw his kindness and doubt and fear and the fullness of his humanity. He thought of his parents and especially of his father **whose jokes** had managed to make him laugh in spite of whatever problems he was having.

He thought of his mother. Of her care and of her dedication to her patients and her kindness. He thought of his love of flying his homemade kites which he would unravel into the wind and watch them morph into a living creature born of his hands yet belonging to the sky. He saw its vibrant colours and felt the tug and pull of it as it sought to climb higher and higher.

Zerach thought of his parents. Of their patience and devotion to him even as they faced what they thought was his illness. They'd been wrong but they had never given up. He thought of the joys of sport. Of the flash of the white ball against the green of the cricket pitch and the sweet spot on his cricket bat as it sent the ball over the boundary for six runs.

He thought of the magnificence of trees, of birds whose wings, like honeyed gold would flutter through the air – joyful and oblivious of their beauty thus making them perfect. He smelt the perfume of the tang of a gum tree and the creatures that lived in it. Of the bats, and owls and the smaller creatures that scurried about their lives, busy with their own minute world.

He felt the snort of a horse as it blew into his nostrils as it flanks quivered with power yet would still allow him to ride it – a bond of trust between two species. He thought too, of the myriad creatures of the land and of the sea, of their abundance, beauty and diversity. Above all he thought of the wonder of creation itself.

He looked to see where Darcy was. The coils had receded a little but he knew it was not enough. 'It's starting to work but we have to try harder. Keep thinking of anything that gives you joy. Visualise it in as much detail as possible. Try to focus on the minutia of what you are imaging. It will make it more real.'

He entered into their minds. He saw what they saw. It was beauteous and in spite of Darcy's plight he felt a fleeting moment of happiness. So many different and unexpected things. Things that he would never have guessed about any of them.

He urged them on with his mind. They would not be aware of his new ability but he was no longer surprised at what he had become. He knew that shortly he would be called on to do a task far harder than this. It would be one that would transform him.

He watched them change their images. The smell of freshly made bread. The smile of a baby. The laughter one shared with family and friends. The eyes of dolphins that looked at you with such deep knowledge it was unnerving. The swoop of a falcon. The song of a bird. The buzzing of bees. The flight of butterflies as they hovered like angels above the flowers.

Centimetre by centimetre the creature was being overcome. It could not deal with the delights of this world. Yes there was pain and sorrow and massive injustices but, in spite of this, beauty was everywhere.

He felt it struggle. The coils were slipping. What had climbed to Darcy's shoulders was now beneath his knees. It tried harder. Forced its darkness into the boy but the images were now starting to blind it.

'Bombard it! Flood it with the images of your minds.' They responded, caught in the wonder of the delight of what they were seeing. Zerach knew it was time. He merged their minds into one. Each of them could see what the others had imagined. They were awash with the magnificence of what they had conjured up. The group had become, for a few seconds, a single mind – a mind that had one purpose, to save their friend.

'Open your eyes,' he said to their minds and look at what you have done.' They opened their eyes and saw Darcy stumbling towards them. He reached them and fell. They grabbed him and held him to them in their embrace.

'I thought that I was going to die,' he said.

'You'll need to rest but we don't have much time,' said Zerach. We need to pack our bags and get the next flight back to Adelaide.'

'But you saw what happened!' exclaimed Thomas. 'We can defeat it. I know we can. Look what you did. You were in our minds. I could feel you.

'I know that you felt our strength but realistically it was a victory of sorts but it's not destroyed'

'But why? Zerach asked Darcy. 'All of you saved me. Together we can stop its invasion of New Zealand.'

'No we can't. I know now that once it gets into a country it's too late.'

'But we're leaving without having done anything! Why did we have to come here at all?' Scarlett asked.

'I think that we needed to see it for ourselves. Now, we have some idea of what we have to face.' He also knew that they must defeat it or die.

CHAPTER THIRTY THREE

They craned forward trying to get a better view of Adelaide from the window of the plane. 'It seems so little and safe,' Scarlett said and although the others said nothing they all felt much the same. It was, however, the safety of the ignorant, for they all knew that eventually if they did not stop the spread of the blackness, Adelaide too would be consumed.

They caught a cab to Scarlett's house and were greeted by Ms. Sayed who looked as tired as they all felt. "The mist of darkness that you saw is spreading rapidly in ChristChurch. As Zerach told you, once it has its hold on a particular country, it is too late to stop it. Your next step will be the hardest and you don't have to travel anywhere.'

'But surely we can't sit here and do nothing. You said that eventually Adelaide would be a target. We have to do something,' Scarlett said.

'You will Scarlett. You will travel a great distance but you won't leave the country.'

'How? Ms. Sayed? How can we do anything stuck here?'

'You have discovered something of the creature or whatever it is that you want to call it. There is unfortunately only one way for you to conquer it. No wait. Conquer isn't the right word. It can never really be destroyed but it can be contained and made to go back from whence it came. That's where you must go.'

'Do you mean . . . do you mean . . .' Darcy stammered, 'that we have to . .. to . . .'

'Yes. You will have to meet it in its own domain. You must leave your bodies and go into its realm. It is, as you know, a realm of darkness, of nothingness, of a void that is so far beyond your imagination that it is impossible to describe. It has no beginning and no end. It is beyond time and space, yet it exists.

It once had form and it was magnificent but it chose another path. That, however, is not your concern. It will try to suck you into its vast emptiness and make you part of the darkness. A place that even light cannot escape from. You must send it back. Can you agree to let your souls travel to a place that will imperil you all? Do you understand what I'm asking of you? my precious ones?'

She waited for them to say something but they sat unmoving and incredulous. 'You have at the most two days to make up your minds. I will look after your mother and Elliot and Fletcher. The rest is now up to you. I wish there was another way but there isn't. You must decide quickly for the darkness will continue to spread.

They saw her hesitate as if she wanted to say more but she silently left the room and softly closed the door. They looked at Zerach waiting for him to speak. 'We'll rest here for two days and build up our strength. Then we'll go to the Botanic Gardens.'

'Why there?' Thomas said.

'The tropical conservatory is like a jungle. Remember it struck first in the Amazon and the conservatory is the closest thing that we have that's like that.'

He'd expected a babble of responses but they sat silently and he was reminded of the expression that he had seen of the faces of soldiers before they went to war. The two days passed quickly and too soon they sat in the car park outside of the Botanic Gardens.

They climbed out of the car and walked along the magnificent avenue of Moreton Bay Figs. The trees' limbs arched over the avenue and it felt to them that they were walking in a leafy cathedral.

They arrived at the giant glass structure with its glass dome under which the trees and plants flourished. Three large trees scraped the top of the dome and the rich green understory of plants gave out a rich smell of humus.

They followed Zerach and he approached a small bridge which arched over a limpid pool of blue water. As they stood there the mist came down from the top of the conservatory and settled onto the leaves and the water formed small Droplets of water.

Each of them inhaled the richness of the soil and the special sense that came with being in a place that felt sacred. 'This is where our physical bodies will stay but our souls won't.'

'How do we do that? Thomas asked.

'When we were in Christchurch we melded our minds. We do it again. In the void, time doesn't exist. When we return to the garden no time will have passed. Ready?' he asked.

CHAPTER THIRTY FOUR

The first shock was that they had no bodies. They were spirits who had dared enter into the lair of the Prince of Darkness, a being so ancient as to be incomprehensible. The second was that there was no sound. It was a void in every sense of the word. No light, no matter how dim, entered. No sense of gravity. No up and no down. No inner and no outer. Eternal space had no dimensions. There was no middle. No direction. It was pure nothingness and it entered into them, eager that at last it was about to defeat these pathetic humans who knew nothing except the ramblings of idiots who spoke of the joy of creation.

How it hated the very word, each syllable in it, emphasised everything that it loathed. Before the creation it was one with the void. Then, billions of years ago, it felt a shudder. A rift had desecrated the void. It saw the formation of stars, of suns, of galaxies and of worlds. Suns shone, spewing out light and heat into the universe. Finally there was the slow formation of planets.

At first they were like him, dark and foreboding, but then, out of underwater vents a blue planet formed an amoeba and then two. They continued to divide and life slowly began to form. Clouds and rain and strange grasses grew and creatures with legs wandered the earth. The blue oceans were now full of life. The blue planet exploded in a madness of creative energy and had continued to evolve.

Worse was to come. A creature formed and lived in the hateful trees. Finally they emerged and stood upright. Then, horror of horrors these creatures developed a glimmer of intelligence. Yet to its rage more was to come. As millions of years went by the creatures left their jungles and ventured out to the savannah. They developed a sense of self coupled with the ability to reason and to plan. They were aware and full of fear, yet now they experienced a sense of wonder. They knew sorrow, joy, and worse of all they knew of love. How it hated them as they continued to populate the earth. How it loathed the colours of life, the birds, the fish and the millions of beings that teemed with life on this planet.

These idiot children had dared to come to his realm believing that they could actually stop him from smothering the earth with its essence. Soon their blue planet would be black-a miniature replica of its own void. After the blue planet, it would turn all of the other planets into blackness. The beings on these planets would perish and it would rejoice as it systematically destroyed all of the worlds that had been created. It would expand its realm throughout the universe and it would be surrounded by dead and silent worlds circling dead suns. Thus it would create perfection. It would claim what was its right. A universal void that would last for eternity.

It looked at the four fools as they faced it and decided to amuse itself. It chose to use their primitive language with its harsh discordant sounds that defiled its perfect quietness. 'The human you call Darcy is already doomed. He was partially mine as I coiled around him and rejoiced in his terror. Now he is mine. You are welcome to observe my powers. Would you like to witness what I can do?'

He felt them resist. How noble of them to try to protect a fellow fool. 'Ah you work as a team, a team comprised of dolts who think they are heroes. Is that the best that you can do? I had expected more of you. The prophecies were so sure, and yet here you are with your feeble minds daring to face me.'

Although Darcy was fighting against it the effort was tearing him apart. It was as if each atom in his body was being rent into millions of shards that flew and disappeared into the void. Soon, he would be too weak to resist. In spite of his agony he managed to reinforce the linking of their minds. He felt their efforts to aid him and he knew that the creature was now focussing on him and that it had dismissed the others as mere minnows.

'Ah I see you're game. A game of chess for five pieces and you are the pawns. How appropriate. You thought that I didn't know that you can meld your minds but what you saw as my oversight was a ruse. A little trick on my part. A ploy. A game that even when played with fools, amused me. You thought you'd pull him back. The hope you felt was exquisite. You are even more foolish than I thought. So easily duped into thinking you had bested me.

Come to me, Darcy my child of darkness. Come to me and be one with me and the void. I will let you be part of a wholeness that you have longed for all of your life. Remember the times when your father used to beat you? Oh how you suffered! I felt your pain and sense of abandonment. Soon you will be healed. You, like me, will be whole and perfect. Come little one come.'

He tried to resist but they knew that he was being drawn in. Somehow, the tendrils that had snaked up his legs had infected him and he was more easily manipulated. Zerach felt his terror as did the others and they reinforced their efforts to stop what was happening.

'Now you're so called perfect four will become the fractured three. Three pawns playing a game that you cannot possibly win. The prophecy was always doomed but I'll enjoy it as the three of you flay about whilst mourning for the loss of my adopted son.' Again it laughed. It was a laugh as black as its domain and it reverberated in them and they felt the crush of it weight as it started to drain away their hope.

'Try harder!' Zerach implored but in spite of their combined minds Darcy was still being inexorably being drawn into the void. Again they felt its triumph as they urged Darcy to resist but they knew that he was vanishing into the void. By now he seemed incapable of responding. Worse, his terror began to lessen. They felt him grow closer to the creature who he was beginning to believe that it wasn't the enemy but someone who loved him. It was what Darcy had yearned for his whole life. He stopped struggling and reached out and embraced his saviour.

They were too stunned to react. Zerach felt their numbing shock and grief. He tried to comfort them but he knew that they were beyond comfort. All of their embryonic courage and actions had led to this. He felt Scarlett's horror and disbelief. Her friend had gone and she hadn't been able to stop him. Zerach knew that she'd believed that her love of Darcy would help but it too had failed.

Zerach felt the beginning of their anguish. He knew that they needed to use the tactics that they'd employed against it when they were in Christchurch. He felt them as they brought forth their images of the abundance of life on the earth. He combined all of their images that shimmered with joy and then attacked the creature hoping the bombardment would overwhelm it. He felt the creature sneer and its voice mocked what they were trying to do.

'You caught me off guard when we were on your blue planet but if you think your pathetic picture collage is going to bring my child back to you you are comically wrong. Trees and flowers and pretty pictures of kittens playing in a field aren't going to make me give up my son. You are deluding yourselves. Now I have one child why not another one? Perhaps Darcy would like the company of the girl with the Scarlett hair. I sense their fondness for each other. Such virtue should be rewarded.'

'Zerach, it's stronger now,' Thomas said. 'I think that as the world gives way to its destruction it grows in power. You have to fight his power with yours.'

'I can't seem to use my power very well in the creature's realm. I made a mistake. I made an assumption that has caused Darcy to be taken from us. I'm sorry. I led you all into this and you trusted me. Not only have I not succeeded I've also lost Darcy.'

'Think of something Zerach! The longer that Darcy is being controlled by the creature the harder it's going to be to get him back.' Zerach knew that Thomas was right but what could he do? It came to him slowly and he was hesitant to say it but he knew that he must. 'We risk destroying ourselves but there is a way. Are you prepared to do it?' Zerach asked. Their response was immediate. They would do it even if it meant their destruction.

Zerach knew that he was drawing on a power so vast he was unsure if he could withstand it, but try he would. His blue light grew brighter and was joined by the other thee. His blue light mingled with the colours of the rainbows of the world and all other worlds. As he did huge flashes of flame shone out of him. He was a beacon of light and they were his satellites. Each of them pulsated at different frequencies and they felt the dark presence of the creature. This time it did not mock or engage in banter. It knew that its adversary had altered. They had harnessed a power that it had not suspected they possessed. The effort of keeping the boy was growing harder but yet it hung on hungry for the boy they called Darcy.

'Give us back Darcy,' Zerach demanded. The creature said nothing. They grew closer to it and, even though it resisted, it could not withstand their light. It was then they saw Darcy. The creature tried another tactic. Suddenly another Darcy appeared and then another. The creature was hiding Darcy in these phantoms that now numbered in their thousands.

Scarlett and Thomas scanned the space that was full of replicas of Darcy. They looked into Zerach's mind and he into theirs. They began to sing. The song was for Darcy. Their song echoed that of the spheres and the ethereal music they made caused the creature to shudder. The spheres were the first beings that The One had created and their power was immense.

They continued singing the Song of the Stars and then the Song of the Universe itself. The creature reeled back but still, it refused to give Darcy up. Again and again they sang. They sang the song whose music was there at the formation of the Universe. It was part of The One and its sacred tones were so rich in nuance and beauty that the stars danced in joy. 'Darcy you need to look into yourself and link with us. Sing with us Darcy. Sing the Song of Songs. It is the music of the universe and it resides in you.'

The creature's resistance was starting to affect it. It began to break apart and splinters of its darkness flew past them. One by one the false Darcy's that had been created began to disappear A shadow began to emerge. His progress was slow and painful. 'Darcy come to us,' they sang. Notes they had never heard before formed perfect harmonies and the void recoiled. The creature was in agony. The music and the melodic harmonies had become too much for it to bear. Slowly it began to withdraw. It would not risk destroying itself for the sake of one of these creatures. It would focus on its rampage of death on the blue planet. Let these fools return to a planet of dust and hopelessness. It withdrew itself and Darcy raced forward to greet them.

'It's time to return,' Zerach said. We have learnt the song of the universe. It is a song that humanity has forgotten but a time will come when they will once again learn it and the world will be transformed.'

'Do you know how we get back?' Darcy asked.

'We follow the song lines. They will show us the way. Meld your minds as strongly as you can. With our combined gifts we will follow the path home.'

They looked around them. They could see the vastness of the universe. It was impossible to comprehend that they were looking at millions galaxies of which their own Milky Way was but one.

At last they saw their planet that hung in space: a blue gem that urged them forward. Finally they could recognise the continents. They saw forests, mountains, rivers and animals that still roamed the plains of Africa as they had for thousands of years.

Suddenly they saw themselves on the little wooden bridge exactly as they had been before they'd left. 'We're home!' Scarlett whispered. She hugged Darcy tightly but he gently pushed her away. 'I don't think I deserve a hug. I was one of the four but I did nothing. All I did was get ensnared by the creature and the three of you had to drag me back. I was bloody useless.'

'No,' Thomas said. 'You were the key that unlocked the full potential of Zerach's power. It was in trying to reach you that we learnt the Song of the Universe. It was that song that saved us.'

'Really? A key? Me?'

'Yes, Darcy you. Be proud of your role and of your race. They've had song lines for thousands of years.' They watched him as he struggled to comprehend the role he'd unknowingly played. 'Darcy, alias The Key,' he said. He laughed and a small woman walked past them and smiled. They were safe. They had returned and the prophecy would gradually begin.

'I think it's time to go back to Scarlett's' Zerach said. 'It's time to begin the change that will heal our planet.

'Just like that?' Thomas said.

'We use the music we learnt. We'll sing it to the world and some will listen and some won't. Even though it may take centuries the songs will be remembered. Some will try to destroy the songs. They will be afraid to let go of what they believe. One day however, all of earth will know The Song and sing the music of the heavens. We won't be here to hear them but the universe will. They'll hear the voices coming from the earth and the planet will rejoice. His words were true, but none of them knew the terrible price that would have to be paid.

ABOUT THE AUTHOR

Noel Morrison is the author of three other novels which have been well received by his readers. He has worked as a Secondary teacher for over thirty years and has a master's degree in counselling.

He lives in rural South Australia and is currently completing masters in theology. He is married with two children and has two grandchildren. He is currently working on his latest fantasy novel 'Medrig the Magician.'